THE TEMPLATE

A PARABLE OF THE ENVIRONMENT

Mark W. Schwiebert

ARCHWAY
PUBLISHING

Archway Publishing books may be ordered through booksellers or by contacting:

Archway Publishing
1663 Liberty Drive
Bloomington, IN 47403
www.archwaypublishing.com
1 (888) 242-5904

Because of the dynamic nature of the Internet, any web addresses or links contained in this book may have changed since publication and may no longer be valid. The views expressed in this work are solely those of the author and do not necessarily reflect the views of the publisher, and the publisher hereby disclaims any responsibility for them.

This is a work of fiction. All characters in this work are fictional. Any resemblance to real persons, living or dead, is coincidental.

ISBN: 978-1-4808-2500-0 (sc)
ISBN: 978-1-4808-2498-0 (hc)
ISBN: 978-1-4808-2499-7 (e)

Library of Congress Control Number: 2015920822

Print information available on the last page.

Archway Publishing rev. date: 1/20/2016

To My Wife, Debbie, whose
support and encouragement are deeply valued

CONTENTS

THE TEMPLATE

"Teach your children what we have taught our children: that the Earth is our Mother. Whatever befalls the Earth befalls the sons and daughters of the Earth. This we know. All things are connected like the blood that unites one family."

– Chief Seattle

TEMPLATE: (a) a pattern or gauge, such as a thin metal plate with a cut pattern, used as a guide in making something accurately; (b) A piece of stone or timber used to distribute weight or pressure evenly.

CHAPTER 1
DISCOVERY

The phone rang at 7:30 Sunday night. Special Agent Derrick Bone was just sitting down to a late meal of fried chicken and biscuits with gravy – a weekly treat in which the usually disciplined triathlete indulged.

"Derrick, you need to come in right away. Something's happened and I want you on it".

Normally reserved and unemotional, the Chief's voice tonight sounded taut. In his quarter century with the F. B. I., Bone had learned to notice little things. "It's not just the devil, but the deadly that's in the details", he frequently admonished Bureau trainees. And tonight, District Director Simpson's voice told him something serious had occurred in which details would be critical.

Within the F.B.I. hierarchy, Bone was something of an anomaly. Considered by his peers a first rate investigator, he had passed up numerous opportunities for the advancement coveted by younger agents, in favor of what he affectionately referred to as "grunt level work". Dogged in his persistence of leads, he wasn't the most popular or political of agents – a fact he wore as a badge of pride. Unafraid of ruffling feathers, some of his superiors balked at assigning him high profile cases, though Director Simpson hadn't yet exhibited this timidity. What the Director had seen during his first year on the job was that Bone was a rock solid, creative detective with a bloodhound's nose for smelling out clues and finding perpetrators.

Arriving twenty minutes later at the F. B. I. branch office in Grand Rapids, Bone was informed by Simpson that he needed to head immediately to Friendship Heights near Holland, Michigan, to take over investigating an incident earlier that evening.

Friendship Heights was the home of former President Joshua Johnson. A Nobel prize-winning Michigander, Johnson had rebounded from his defeat for reelection after a single term by becoming one of the foremost humanitarians in the world. Each summer, he returned from his global undertakings to his "cottage" at Friendship Heights overlooking Lake Michigan. There he spent a month in reflection and "getting back to his roots", as he put it.

President Johnson's visibility had increased dramatically over the preceding eighteen months as he led the charge for major changes in global environmental policy. Although Michigan, with its manufacturing base anchored in fossil-fuel vehicles, would have been expected to take poorly to its favorite son's efforts, his deep devotion to his home state's natural beauty and resources had tempered local reaction and even garnered widespread support in his political backyard.

Now Director Simpson informed Derrick that the former President was dead. He had been discovered about 7:00 p.m. by his Secret Service detail face down in the water near the boat dock below the main house at Friendship Heights. A helicopter had been put at Derrick's disposal to get him to the ten acre site quickly. Simpson told him little, as Simpson himself knew little at this point. Besides, he reflected, Bone will take this investigation in whatever direction his nose leads. And whatever I tell him won't make much difference anyway.

While Bone choppered to Friendship Heights, he mentally

reviewed what he knew of the former President. He recalled, among other things, that Johnson was a devoted outdoorsman who was an excellent swimmer, delighting in ending his summer days in Michigan with a vigorous lengthy swim out from his dock and back again.

Although the initial report from Holland suggested the President died of a heart attack, being an ex-President prompted a more thorough investigation than may have been initiated for "mere mortals", as the Chief drily put it. Simpson also informed Derrick the President had undergone a thorough physical exam at the Mayo Clinic in Minnesota just a month earlier. And, as reported at the time by the media, the exam revealed a sixty-year old man with the body of a thirty-five year old.

Bone also vaguely recalled reading a couple of articles about the ex-President's heavy involvement in peace negotiations awhile before in some volatile parts of Africa where every tribe and ethnic group seemed to have a grievance against its neighbor. Certain global leaders, including the current President, had at that time, sought out Johnson's help as a result of his precedent-shattering work in brokering a previously elusive peace deal between Israel and the P.L.O several years earlier.

Derrick also knew the ex-President's advocacy for environmental reform took up the crusade started by former Vice President Al Gore following his own failed effort to gain the White House in 2000. But Derrick had not followed Johnson's activities closely – his obsession with F.B.I. work and limited interest in politics prevented this. He did, however, know that Johnson's ideas, though often controversial, generally struck him as pretty well grounded in fact and common sense.

He also recalled there had been some backlash to Johnson's

initiatives. Bone's impression was that most of them came from "Right Wing Nuts", a term for certain radio talk show hosts an ex-girlfriend coined and left with Derrick, along with the locket containing his picture and a "Dear John" letter she'd given him ending their bumpy relationship.

He considered what motive someone might have for going after a person dedicated to working for peace and a cleaner environment. He could think of any number of possibilities. For every "do-gooder", he mused, there are half a dozen "do-nothings" and four or five "no-gooders". Still, at the moment, there seemed no obvious suspects – if foul play was involved at all.

Agent Bone mulled these meager facts as his chopper descended to the grounds of Friendship Heights. Given his background, he tended to view the world with a suspicious eye, looking for hidden meanings or darker purposes where none necessarily existed. He periodically had to curb this tendency. What worked well in solving crimes could be annoying socially. More than one woman he'd felt drawn to walked away in frustration after realizing his obsession with crime and generally dark outlook on human nature. Bone himself ultimately rationalized his skepticism as an occupational asset; more useful than not in unraveling the plots of those bent on twisting circumstances to their own criminal advantage. As a result, Derrick's social life for many years had shown about as much life as the numerous corpses he was called upon to examine.

The chopper touched down on the evergreen shrouded lawn of Friendship Heights fifteen minutes after leaving Grand Rapids. The press had already started to gather, drawn like vultures by news of the ex-President's death. The normally tranquil and darkening hillsides of the retreat were ablaze with the lights of arriving vans carrying high powered flood lights intended to frame reporters giving news on the breaking story.

Bone was met at the edge of the security perimeter surrounding the beachfront property by his old friend, Secret Service Agent Monty Le Beau. With him was another Secret Service Agent Le Beau introduced as Dick Rodman. Rodman acted aloof, seemingly resentful the F. B. I. had been called in, since it implied commission of a crime on his watch. Le Beau, however, was more forthcoming.

"Glad you could get here so soon, Derrick. I specifically asked your new branch Chief - what's his name? Oh yeah, Simpson, to have you detailed here. We've secured the area; and arrangements have been made for an autopsy to be performed in Grand Rapids." The usually steady Le Beau sounded slightly rattled, Derrick thought. All the normally cool heads are nervous tonight.

Bone, always restless with small talk, cut to the point: "Tell me what happened and what you first observed when you found Johnson."

"Well, about 7:00 p.m., the former President headed down to the lake for his usual swim. Nothing seemed out of the ordinary. Same thing he'd do every night. We'd accompany him to the dock and have a patrol boat off shore in case anything happened. He hated security and insisted the boat keep its distance so he didn't have to inhale the fumes from the engine while he was swimming. Said he'd prefer the agents use a rowboat instead of a 'stinkpot' - as he called the outboard. We'd tell him the outboard was needed in case any thing happened that required speed.

"In any event, he waded into the water and swam a few strokes, then he just stopped. Sometimes he'd do that, if he'd forgotten something or gotten a page on the pager he always insisted on taking with him. So we didn't think too much about it right way. Only he didn't resume swimming for about a minute. Then I ran out on the dock and found him face down in the water. I called for backup and dove in to check on him. He offered no resistance and wasn't responsive. We pulled him out and did C. P. R. All the usual stuff. But he was already gone. Agent Rodman here was in the boat about twenty-five yards offshore, and he did a loop of the swimming area to see if there was any evidence, any suspicious activity in the water. He found nothing.

"We hustled the President to the E. R. in Holland; but, as I said, we pretty well knew he was already gone."

"What area did the boat check?" Bone asked.

"Dick here – Agent Rodman – did a zigzag pattern of the pattern of a semi-circle radius about 50 yards offshore working his way to the dock. The waters were clear and nothing suspicious turned up. No foreign objects, movements, or anything else of interest. I mean the President was a vigorous and active man one minute, and just dead the next."

"It had to be a heart attack", Agent Rodman interjected.

"Yeah. But somehow, something just doesn't smell right", Le Beau continued. "I mean the guy was an avid swimmer and had checked out at Mayo with flying colors a month before".

"Heart attacks happen even to vigorous people with no warning. I've seen it happen with triathletes", Bone mused, playing the devil's advocate.

Le Beau responded, "Yeah - you'd know about that. You still do those crazy races?"

Not waiting for an answer, the Secret Service Agent drew Bone away by the arm. He continued gravely, "Trouble is, President Johnson tended to be pretty obsessive about staying in touch – even to the point of taking his pager with him when he went swimming. Always wanted to be accessible.

He was dead earnest about that". Le Beau paused, "Sorry, bad choice of words."

"Yeah?" Bone responded expectantly.

"Well, tonight when we retrieved his body from the water, the pager was missing".

CHAPTER 2
THE DEBATING SOCIETY

Twenty months earlier:

GENEVA, SWITZERLAND (News Release) Foreign Secretaries of the Big Twelve economic powers, converged on this historic city today to face a matter of as much urgency as that prompting leaders to adopt the Geneva Convention on Military Protocols here a century ago. A rising tide of environmental disasters worldwide – from prolonged droughts in sub-Saharan Africa and the American Southwest to intensified coastal hurricanes in Asia, the Americas, and Europe – has focused attention of world leaders on the growing problem of climate change. The big question here: 'Is it already too late?' The prevailing spirit seems to be it is not. But the very fact the question is being asked underscores the world's growing alarm at how to reverse an accelerating trend of global and environmental disasters.

Helen Michaud, the U. S. Secretary of State, had begun the conference with an address unthinkable from her a year earlier, when official administration policy routinely dismissed warnings of global warming as "hysterical" and "harmful to the national economy". Her comments now openly and

freely acknowledged the reality of the problem, and cited
political and military as well as economic consequences of
the growing number of environmental disasters which had
severely damaged costal areas in the United States from
New England to Southern Florida. To sustained applause,
she cited the unacceptable cost of too much consumption
and too much waste, "both in terms of the future left to our
children and the political turmoil caused between nations
and within nations".

Yet advocates for greater environmental controls still en-
countered a mixed assortment of objectors. Some opposed
any kind of global action; others voiced alarm that more
regulation could cost jobs and reduce standards of living in
developed countries. Rod Churlish, former National Security
Adviser and now a frequent radio talk show guest and syndi-
cated columnist, served as the point man for interest groups
denying environmental problems, by providing a steady diet
of commentary and criticism. Though his links to large oil
and gas companies and to certain large petroleum producing
Arab states were well known, he framed his arguments in
patriotic terms: "Why should we be dictated to by foreign
environmental activists who want to regulate what we drive
or own?", he would argue. "America has always been a land
of big appetites: for adventure, for expansion, and for freedom. We surrender our right to determine our own future
at our peril. We know better what's in our national interests than some global organization, or somebody in some
country whose freedoms were long ago sacrificed on the
altar of creeping socialism. Now they want to take away our
right to choose the cars we want; the size houses we live in;
what we eat and what we wear. I say 'no' to these prophets
of doom and gloom; who claim less is more based on some
half-baked threat of climate change. Our freedoms depend

on our freedom of choice; where we live, what and how much we consume, and what and where we want to drive."

Then without a touch of irony, Churlish blasted America's own elected leaders for making decisions based on America's self-interest when they disagreed with his own: "These populist potentates in Washington sell out our core values of economic expansion by limiting or discouraging consumption. How do they expect us to create jobs and realize the American Dream if they limit what we can buy and how we can reward ourselves for our honest hard work? It's downright un-American. They'll regulate us to death".

Representatives of the O'Brien Administration – newly converted to environmental awareness - sought to counter these and other arguments as the conference in Geneva unfolded. "Connecting the dots" became the primary theme, as the growing string of environmental catastrophes inspiring the conference became "Exhibit A" for those championing reform measures. A series of violent Level 5 hurricanes striking coastal communities from Rio de Janeiro to Charleston, South Carolina had resulted in the displacement of tens of thousands of people and billions of dollars in property damage. Rising ocean levels had resulted in storm surges swamping commercial and cruise ship docking facilities from New York City and Seattle, to Mumbai, India and Capetown, South Africa; causing drastic economic disruption.

The correlation between ocean disasters and global warming – predicted by scientific data since nearly three decades before in the early 90's - were now coming home with a vengeance.

Unfortunately, the magnitude of the problems represented the first and - seemingly last issue on which conferees could agree. The Europeans favored a strict cap on any future fossil fuel omissions, a position to which nations in the European Union had been moving for years. The U. S. and Canada continued to favor a cap and trade system with limits on fossil fuels driven more by market regulation than by strict prohibition. Meanwhile, India and China – with the most to gain or lose in the short term from new global controls on available fuel – supported a two tiered system that allowed expanded use of fossil fuel, paired with government commitments to develop cleaner energy alternatives and even to whole new cities that were carbon neutral.

After five days of meetings, little was accomplished beyond the parties staking out their positions. The official conference communiqué weakly concluded that "a meaningful exchange of positions was shared to lay the foundation for further progress as discussions continue in the near future".

Secretary Michaud, weary of the posturing back and forth over the prior week, candidly shared her disappointment with her close associates on the flight home:

"It will take even more serious disasters than we've already seen to get done what's needed. We may have to see things 'go nuclear' before we see real change".

Little did she realize the prophetic nature of her words.

CHAPTER 3
FLASHPOINT

MOGADISHU, SOMALIA

Sheik Omar was angry. The pirate band he had organized and operated profitably for a decade faced its first serious challenge - and from an infuriating source. It did not come from Western powers, who continued to lamely protest but took little action to protect their freighters off Somali shores. The shipping companies themselves had muzzled resistance, not wanting to politicize a profitable industry by arming crew members or seeking adequate naval protection. Better and cheaper, they reasoned, to pay the occasional ransom, even though it might encourage more piracy.

No, the threat to Sheik Omar instead came from his own ranks. One of his young lieutenants, Hussein Ali, from his own tribe and possessing the same acquisitive appetites, had prevailed upon a gang of pirates based on the northern edge of the horn of Somalia to form their own alliance in rebellion against the Sheik. Promised a larger share of the spoils than Sheik Omar provided, the mutineers seized arms supplies stored in depots from Berbera around the Horn of Africa and south 250 miles; then took over a fleet of swift "cigarette boats" that had become the pirates' tool of choice. Ali had brutally tortured and executed three of Sheik Omar's top deputies in the North, both as a demonstration of his ferocity and out of concern for their continued loyalty to the Sheik.

It was apparent Ali was ready for open warfare with his powerful former boss.

Omar knew what he had to do. If he tolerated the insurrection, it would encourage more. In the tribes of Somalia, the rule of an eye for an eye held sway even more so than in the industrialized West, and the Sheik was eager to apply this principle with overwhelming force to his former subordinate.

The question was how? The Somali government represented no real threat or opportunity. Chronically dysfunctional as the result of droughts which had displaced large portions of the population and created an endless spiral of internal warfare and suffering, the government headquartered in Mogadishu had little influence outside the capital. Efforts at reclaiming farmland ravaged by years of blistering drought had been futile; though it had been optimistically hoped this would accommodate resettlement and resolve at least some of the tribal feuding.

Nor was outside intervention much of a threat: most of the world cared little about Somalia and its fraternal bloodbaths. Indeed, the oil-exporting companies and countries frankly welcomed a feud among the pirates as it might distract and disrupt them from their lucrative piracy business.

What Sheik Omar understood was that such an internal struggle could ultimately have the opposite effect. Struggling over share of booty would cost money, and thus escalate the need for more piracy. Shrewdly, Sheik Omar realized such an action could eventually expand piracy to an unacceptable level, which would inevitably prompt a crackdown and halt his carefully orchestrated operation.

He had no doubt he could crush his underling. But his former lieutenant was brash and unpredictable. He could escalate things in such a way as to provoke the sleeping giant of

Western naval power to crush the Sheik's enterprise, whose growth he'd carefully managed to prevent such a reaction.

What the Sheik needed was something that could end the quarrel with Ali swiftly and decisively. He needed a solution that could make it frighteningly clear to any other challengers that the consequences would be swift and overwhelming. What's more, if he could gain greater status in the region - maybe even globally - so much the better. He would "protect his investment", he slyly smiled, echoing a business ethic he'd heard expressed by so many captains of industry in the West.

Sheik Omar knew it was time to reconnect with allies in Iran and Pakistan to obtain a device that no rebel force could resist. He would obtain a weapon often discussed, but seldom used; powerfully effective and irresistible in magnitude.

He would secure and detonate over Ali's headquarters, a nuclear device that would obliterate his enemies.

Military intelligence in the West, closely monitoring exchanges between Moslem states with nuclear capabilities and their allies, quickly learned of Sheik Omar's intentions through poorly coded transmittals. Back channel communications began avoiding normal routes. Diplomatic relations still didn't exist between Washington and Tehran and were strained with Islamabad. These messages expressed concern that any arms deals or technology transfers to rogue powers, like the Somali pirates, were completely unacceptable and would be met with the gravest response.

The trouble was, after years of belligerent finger-pointing and saber-rattling back and forth between Western and fundamentalist Islamic regimes, such threats held little credibility. The Islamic countries had used oil revenues to build their own economic and trade relationships with growing economies of China and southern Asia. Nations like Malaysia and the Philippines, with large Moslem populations of their own, felt a community of interest with fundamentalist Islamic states that was merely reinforced by resentment toward their former colonial masters in the West. As a leading Moslem mullah in Iran expressed it: "The West has had its day. They had colonization; then they had NATO to force its will on the faithful during the post-colonial period. Now the Nation of Islam will rise again and form its own alliances, for trade, prosperity, and military strength".

The differences between fundamentalist and modern Islamic states remained great. But all could appreciate the advantage of working together.

And so, in an ironic imitation of Western practice, the Moslem nations had founded "I.U.F.P.P." or "Islam United for Prosperity and Propagation". This global alliance built on a common religious identity, counteracted the powerful economic influences of the Western economic powers as well as newer economic powerhouses in China and India.

The West - particularly the United States - still had clout. Foreign aid and the positive influence of U. S. - based charitable organizations assured that. But the accelerating power of technology, which not only gave access to information but heightened risks to security, had exploded access to information and development.

Meanwhile, the prospect of raising the discomfort of ideological foes - while also possibly driving up the cost of fossil oil as the result of global uncertainty - appealed to certain Arab leaders who were experienced at exploiting the West's addiction to fossil fuels.

Former President Johnson occupied an unusual position in this emerging crisis. As an American President, he had initially attracted the suspicion of Moslem leaders. Yet he had sought to build bridges during his four years in office, even negotiating an armistice between Israel and the

Palestinian leadership over the future governance of the city of Jerusalem. This paved the way for a negotiated resolution of broader issues, allowing a peace treaty finally to be agreed upon between Israel and Palestine that had held for the last half decade.

As tensions mounted in Somalia and with it central Asian benefactors, President O'Brien - a moderate Republican whose unlikely nomination occurred after a walk-out by the right wing and Tea Party remnant of the G.O.P. at the 2020 nominating convention - monitored the escalating crisis with growing concern. O'Brien, a likeable fellow in the mold of his hero Ronald Reagan, likened himself to the popular 40th President, while rejecting his "supply side" economics as "nonsense" - at least to his inner circle. He recognized certain aspects of Reaganomics had set the stage for soaring deficits, hobbling U. S. credit and economic growth. O'Brien's relations with his more wonkish predecessor, Joshua Johnson, had been strained. On the environment in particular, the current President initially resented his predecessor's outspoken advocacy of a more rigorous response to climate change and resource depletion. O'Brien privately understood the severity of the problem, but publicly argued any response had to be balanced with its impact on the economy the public could accept. He felt an ex-President should understand this, and Johnson either did and ignored it; or didn't, and was just a trouble maker. "That's why he was a one-termer", O'Brien dryly concluded.

For his part, former President Johnson remained abundantly aware of his political Achilles heel. He was perhaps too much of a scientist to have ever flourished in the political arena. Only half-jokingly he remarked, "Johnsons never did well in the White House. Andrew got impeached. Lyndon got chased out over Vietnam. And I talked painful truth about the environment. We shared a common last name and fate – all one-termers".

But this didn't temper his advocacy. With the possible exception of Jimmy Carter, he was often referred to in the media as the "best Ex-President we ever had".

Now, the current President put a call through to his some-times difficult predecessor.

The secretary placing the call informed the ex that the current President was on the line.

"Joshua, this is Dick."

Taken aback at the unexpected call, Johnson initially paused.

"Mr. President, to what do I owe this unexpected honor?" Johnson then inquired somewhat sardonically.

"Joshua", the current President, continued, choosing to avoid formality and hoping Johnson would take the cue and do likewise.

"I need your help".

"Really". Johnson's voice reflected his surprise. Then collecting himself, he briskly asked "What's up".

"There's a positive shit-fest brewing in Somalia", the plainspoken O'Brien continued. "The damned pirates have gotten themselves in a mini-civil war in which the chief sheik has been challenged by one of his underlings. Now the boss has decided the way to teach his former lieutenant a lesson is by going nuclear. And he's likely to go to Iran or Pakistan to get the weapon. It's part of this whole Pan-Islamic thing sweeping the Arab world. Wanting to flex their muscles and reclaim their caliphate, I guess. Crazy as it may seem, we're afraid the Pakistanis and Iranians may actually do business with this guy, figuring he won't do much damage in the Somali desert. And it would show us they aren't afraid to get tough".

There was a pause at the other end, as the former President absorbed the seemingly impossible: a nuclear incident, dreaded for over seventy-five years since the nuclear arms race began, could now be triggered by a quarrel between a bunch of pirates. At first, it seemed almost laughable. Yet, he reflected, global crises had come from obscure origins before; the assassination of Archduke Franz Ferdinand ignited World War I; and the Cuban Missile Crisis in 1962, nearly set the world ablaze.

In some respects, he reflected it was likely to happen this way. The Superpowers understood what was at stake. A bunch of thugs who make their living off thievery can't be expected to think, especially long term. Besides, they see themselves having little to lose and much to gain.

"What can I do to help?" he quickly responded.

"Well, first of all, I need you to come to Washington to get updated on what's going on over there. Then I need you to go over there and see if you can talk some sense to these people. You've got as good a reputation as any of us 'Christian infidels' - as they call us - and might be able to get through to them".

Johnson ignored O'Brien's disparaging tone towards Moslems. Instead, he cut to the key question: "What tools are you prepared to give me to negotiate?"

President O'Brien was surprised at the bluntness of his predecessor's request. He paused. He hadn't discussed details with his National Security team. Even the call to Johnson would have been discouraged by several of them who thought the ex-President too radical to be trusted. But O'Brien had gone with his instinct and made the call. So now he plowed ahead.

"Well, given the stakes involved, you'd have broad authority to negotiate any kind of deal that could defuse this thing; and ideally get us some better working conditions in this part of the world".

A concept was already emerging in Johnson's mind; an idea he'd been cultivating for the last couple of years without any suitable stage on which to mount it. Now from the current crisis may come the ideal opportunity to implement it with the backing of the U. S. government. He had in mind a program which could potentially transform chronically poor and troubled parts of the globe into regions with a measure of prosperity, while at the same time addressing a major environmental issue.

"I'm on my way," Johnson answered.

CHAPTER 4
SUSPICIONS

After inspecting the beach area and finding little of interest Bone asked to see the President's body. Agent Le Beau reported it had been removed to Trinity Hospital in Grand Rapids for autopsy.

"Who's doing the autopsy?" Bone demanded.

"One of the local pathologists – a Dr. Sidney – is assisting the County Medical Examiner. We're also having one of our guys flown in from Washington."

Bone recognized Sidney as a competent pathologist with whom he'd worked. Still Bone was glad they were bringing in a sawbones from D.C. It would slow things down a little while they waited for him to arrive.

"What did the President have to eat in the twenty-four hours before he died?" Bone asked somewhat off-handedly.

"His usual diet was pretty boring stuff" Le Beau replied. "He'd have dry bran cereal with fresh fruit and vitamins for breakfast; then a sandwich and soup for lunch; and a little heavier meal for dinner, normally after his swim."

"I didn't ask what he usually ate. I asked what foods he ate in his last twenty-four hours." Bone knew his voice had taken on the unfriendly edge that repelled people. But it didn't matter; one of the earliest lessons he'd learned in investigating crimes was that the first twenty-four hours were the most important. It's during that time that material leads would be secured or lost.

"Shit, Derek, I don't know precisely what he had. We can

get a list of what the cook prepared for lunch. Before swimming he'd often have a light snack. Then afterward, at supper
we'd all eat together. President Johnson insisted on it."

"Well, then lets get that information; and whether anyone
had access to the President's food over the last forty-eight
hours."

"What, do you think he was poisoned?"

"Who knows? A normally vigorous 60 year old, accustomed to swimming long distances, drops dead after a few
strokes in the water. Doesn't make any sense. And there are
drugs or chemicals that can simulate a heart attack."

"Well, we'll check the blood as part of the autopsy to
see if there are any traces of any unusual chemicals. But as
to access to his food, his cook had been with the President
since the White House years and was like a member of his
family. He'd even get on us if he thought we weren't doing
something right to protect the Old Man – and you know how
obsessive the Secret Service can be."

"Yeah, I know", Bone replied flatly. He'd had issues with
the Secret Service since they interfered with a murder investigation he'd supervised involving the Scarpati Crime
Syndicate twelve years earlier. When the investigation suggested financial connections between government officials
and syndicate bosses, it had been shut done.

"I want to talk to him anyway."

"Okay, he is pretty cut up already, as close to the President
as he was", Le Beau replied.

"What about motives?" Bone persisted, "Who would want
to see the ex-President dead?"

"Where should we start? He pissed off much of industry
by pushing for alternate, non-fossil fuels. The oil producing
countries, including some pretty nasty states in the Mid-
East that sponsor terrorists, resented his push for fossil fuel

independence. Even some major retailers disliked his talk of doing more with less. That whole <u>Template</u> thing he had been pushing for the last couple of years made a lot of people mad."

Bone had heard about President Johnson's idea of a "<u>Template for Our Time</u>". A set of standards widely billed as a repudiation of rampant Western consumerism that extended back to the post-World War II period and beyond. Bone hadn't paid much attention to the talk, because it didn't affect his own investigations - or, for that matter him personally. He lived what one of his ex-girlfriends described as "the life of a monk crossed with that of a worker bee: work hard, eat little, indulge less, and work some more".

"You wouldn't have to look far to find enemies with motives", Le Beau concluded. "Lots of folks resented the President's ongoing work to do more with less and recycle what we've got."

"Trouble with that theory", Le Beau mused openly, "is that for everyone who has a motive for opposing Johnson, there were PR representatives and repackaging companies seeking to tie in with the new models the ex-President was promoting. Big hardware store chains were peddling 'do it yourself' repair and recycling products; other retailers were pushing new Personal Sustainability Devices, or 'P.S.D.s for use at home or at work to make lifestyles more energy efficient. From solar powered cell phones to roof mounted wind turbines, P.S.D.'s were taking off. Even the big oil companies were getting into the act by using oil profits to develop alternate sustainable energy – like Saudi Arabia promoting solar cells and batteries. It was as if everyone was beginning to see the sense of Johnson's ideas and climbing on board with new ways to exploit them."

"Why Monty, you're almost starting to sound like a

freaking environmentalist yourself." Bones prodded his politically conservative friend.

But the information was useful. Motives could be con-
flicted and as hard to fathom as the suspicious death itself.

"And of course the Right Wing crowd was absolutely
livid at what President Johnson was trying to do", Le Beau
continued, ignoring his FBI colleague.

"They called the former President everything from
'un-American' to 'traitor' and all things in between. But like
a lot of what the media says, it was all gas and no action."

Bone interrupted his friend's musings, "Did you locate
the President's pager?"

"Oh, yeah", Le Beau responded "We found it in the shallow water near the dock. Seems it had peeled off the Velcro
belt Johnson usually wore when he was swimming. Probably
dropped off as he walked into the water. The fastener on
the belt pouch that carried it had separated, allowing it to
fall out."

"That ever happen before?"

"Nope, Johnson would have had a fit if it had. He kept
that pager on him wherever he went. Almost seemed superstitious about it."

"Did you fingerprint it?"

Le Beau paused embarrassed. "Well, no I guess we didn't
yet. When we got him out of the water we removed the strap
on his waist. The water could affect fingerprints anyway."

Bone glared at him, "Fingerprint it anyway, especially
the pouch."

Then almost on impulse, he ordered, "And when they do
the autopsy, tell them to save some of the President's blood."

CHAPTER 5
NEGOTIATION

The briefing at the White House went remarkably well. President O'Brien, keen on preventing the "Tempest in a Teapot", as he referred to the Somali crisis, from erupting into the first hostile nuclear action since Nagasaki, silenced Johnson's enemies in the Administration. He also promised his predecessor latitude to negotiate a reasonable deal - subject to Presidential sign off - for up to two billion dollars. The key point - and on this the two President's were in full agreement - was that any solution could not be seen as a payoff; but as means to foster basic political reform in the historically unstable Horn of Africa. From the current President's perspective, he wanted to avoid disruption of oil supplies and defuse tension in a troubled part of the Moslem world. For the former President, there was also the chance to take a "lemon and make lemonade" on both economic and environmental fronts. He described his plan to President O'Brien, who was skeptical, but signed off anyway, recognizing his options were limited. President Johnson was, after all, the only ace O'Brien's had up this particular sleeve.

In a curious reversal of roles, the former President initiated contacts with Sheik Omar and the Somali government instead of the U.S. State Department.

President Johnson had cultivated friendships with a number of Moslem heads of state, who viewed him as a political anomaly: a former President of the United States with the prestige that titled carried, but one focused with almost religious intensity on securing a more peaceful and just world. Johnson came from a Christian rather than Moslem background; but his devoutness was sincere and unencumbered by the doctrinal narrowness of certain Christian or Moslem fundamentalists. This actually seemed to create a bond between him and many Mideast leaders for whom religion - whether out of personal conviction or political necessity - was central to their conduct. Add to this Johnson's success in brokering the long elusive Israeli-Palestinian peace deal, and his standing among Arab leaders was considerable.

A Syrian intermediary set up the initial meeting between Johnson and Sheik Omar. The Syrians had provided aid to the pirates for years. More to the point, Syria had in the past facilitated transfer of nuclear technology into some pretty questionable hands. So, as Johnson put it, they needed to put some skin in the game and, given the circumstances, could either be the hero or the goat.

The initial meeting convened in Damascus - at the Center for Creative Islamic Diplomacy. Sheik Omar arrived with a retinue of hungry looking Somali bandits dressed uncomfortably for the occasion in costly, ill-fitting western suits but wearing traditional Arab head- dress. Former President Johnson showed up accompanied only by his scientific and personal assistant, Dr. Lydia Stonecraft, a fellow Midwesterner with advanced degrees in biological engineering and physics from the University of Illinois. The Somali President, beleaguered and isolated in his own capital, showed up alone.

The meeting was set up with utmost confidentiality. Public knowledge of the nuclear issue could have created a media frenzy; and O'Brien didn't want to openly embrace Johnson or his initiatives until he had a better idea that his ideas would bear fruit. The Syrians similarly sought a low profile pending favorable results. And the Sheik, sensing the possibility of a lucrative deal, was willing to sheath his sword, at least temporarily, in the hope of a deal that could cost him little and gain much.

The Syrian Foreign Minister hosting the meeting began with the customary rituals and courtesies attending any Mideast conference. Tea and biscuits were circulated with polite conversation that extended for three-quarters of an hour.

President Johnson, knowing the urgency of the circumstances and how these matters progressed, participated in the rituals respectfully. He understood that wars had been started or avoided based on the direction these seemingly innocuous introductory rituals followed.

After forty-five minutes of delicate conversations about the virtues of the Foreign Secretary's distinguished family and the honorableness of honest fishermen (now pirates) in the Horn of Africa, matters finally moved to the issues at hand.

Foreign Secretary Hassad signaled that formal discussions could begin when he observed that it was the disruption of fishing opportunities off the Horn of Africa that had first triggered the Somali "naval actions" - his polite spin on raw acts of piracy.

President Johnson acknowledged this was true. He ceded historic opportunities by the coastal people of Somalia had changed. Not only were other nations encroaching on traditional Somali fishing waters, but the supply of fish itself had been depleted by over-fishing.

However, he concluded, "It would take many years to reverse this, because the natural balance God – Allah - intended has been disturbed over many years by the acts of us all".

The allusion to God or Allah, seemed to please his

listeners. It was one of the levels on which Johnson connected with leaders in the Middle East. Being "called" by God - though known by different names - stimulated political action in this part of the world. And here the case was made that God, or Allah, had endowed us with bounty which our own overuse had depleted.

Johnson continued, "Yet, though conditions have changed, new opportunities have thrust themselves upon us. If we are wise, we may uplift our people, and be affirming to our God's will, as well."

Sheik Omar and the silent President of Somalia, both looked interested if a little perplexed at where the former leader of the Free World was going. President Johnson would not keep them waiting long. It felt as if he had been waiting for this opportunity for years.

Johnson pressed forward: "The Horn of Africa - and indeed much of the northern half of the African continent - is richly blessed with two inexhaustible gifts: sunlight and open land". He might have said desert instead of "open land"; but that would have stated the obvious and seemed discourteous. It also would have undercut the point he was about to make.

"Off the Horn of Africa, we have a third resource in abundance; the ocean."

Then he continued, "Our Earth absorbs ten thousand times the energy each year from the sun than all of humanity currently needs. Much of that energy – both from heat and light – falls on regions like Somalia. You see, it is not just oil that makes the Middle East rich in energy resources." Johnson added with a wry smile.

"The difference, of course, is that we haven't figured out how to capture and store the sunlight's energy as efficiently as we have with oil and gas. But sunlight also doesn't produce greenhouse gases which threaten the future of our children and grandchildren.

"So even though we know how to tame the sun; we haven't done much of it because it has been easier to use fossil fuels to power our machines, our boats, and our buildings.

"But consider", he paused longer than needed for the translation, "what if we were to build huge pumps on the coast of Somalia to convey millions of gallons of seawater to solar powered plants on the Somali coast or inland. Then, by heat and evaporation we could produce fresh water. This would be used to irrigate crops in what is now empty desert. We could allow the deserts to blossom, producing food and building materials Somalia badly needs. We could, at the same time, reduce greenhouse gases by gobbling up CO_2 with the crops grown for harvest. And the salt and other minerals produced through evaporation of sea water could be processed for other uses – from skin products to industrial chemicals. The crops needed to feed Somalia; jobs needed to employ Somalians; and exportable products valued to support Somalia's recovery – all could be secured in a manner that would help, not hurt, God's creation. And all this could be done by using natural resources Somalia largely already possesses in abundance."

President Johnson paused. His enthusiasm for ideas could be infectious. He also knew that he could overwhelm his listeners and lose them with his leaps of reason. Given the cultural reserve of his host and fellow conferees, he waited to gauge their reaction. The Sheik and Somali President glanced at each other warily, waiting for the other to speak first. The Syrian Foreign Minister broke the silence with words calculated in their diplomacy yet crafty in their practicality.

"This is a very interesting idea, Mr. President. It offers much our whole region needs to consider since all our countries have much sun and, as you delicately put it, 'open land'". But we have built hydroponic plants before in desert regions and they are costly. It is very costly to produce the kinds of water you need for your proposal."

Johnson was direct. "I bring with me certain assurances from the President of the United States regarding financial assistance to help overcome these obstacles. Naturally, costs are always a concern; but I believe the United States would have an active and meaningful interest in not only addressing the current conflict in this part of the world; but in providing a model that could be used through much of Saharan Africa and in coastal regions all around the World."

Then he added pointedly, "However, as many Moslem nations share an interest in resolving the current crisis and in fostering greater wealth and stability to this region, we would expect sister Mideast nations - including your own Mr. Foreign Secretary" he said looking directly at the Syrian Foreign Secretary, " to play a significant financial part as well."

The Sheik spoke up next, "What benefit would these plans have for my people, who are fisherman and live on the coast? They are not farmers and have no interest in the desert."

They're not fisherman anymore either, President Johnson thought to himself. Just pirates.

But instead he looked the Sheik directly in the eye and said evenly, "I fully understand what you say. But the reason your followers have changed their traditional livelihood from fishing to …other occupations, is because their traditional way of life was no longer profitable. Fish stocks are diminished due to overfishing - even if we expand protection to your territorial waters. But what we are talking about here is a new industry and range of opportunities for your people; from building solar plants in coastal areas to operating them, to pursuing a variety of jobs in the expanding economy of your nation.

"What's more," he added, revealing an understanding of the Sheik's implicit concern, "Your personal role in this new industry would be significant, as a leader in organizing support and as an investor receiving a steady and reliable dividend from ever growing resources Somalia would gain from its expanding economy. And your enemy would become increasingly irrelevant as Somalia gained more reliable income and occupations. Besides, you know it is a matter of time before shipping interests crack down on high seas 'adventurism' like your enemy pursues."

The Somali President, still listening cautiously, appeared to be listening intently and leaned toward the former President as he continued speaking. He finally saw a ray of hope for his beleaguered and ravaged country.

The negotiations continued for the balance of the day and into the following week with interruptions for only meals and sleep. By the end of the second day, general terms had been agreed to for an establishment of the "Somali Power and Resource Enterprise" to be overseen by the Somali government in tandem with international representatives of the U.S. and several Mideast countries including Syria and Saudi Arabia. Its stakeholders would include the Sheik and other key tribal leaders from inland Somalia whose largely barren territories would be needed for the growing fields. Iran and Pakistan with pressure from both Shiites and Sunni Islamic leaders, backed away from nuclear intrigue to lend financial support to a promising new model for transforming historically impoverished equatorial Moslem countries into self-supporting economies.

Perhaps not surprisingly given the cloak of secrecy surrounding the meetings and relatively obscure part of the world, little public attention was aroused by the transformational process unfolding in Damascus. But, key leaders in the Mideast were aware of a nuclear crisis averted. They also recognized the global significance of the model Johnson had proposed if it proved successful.

Former President Johnson's image within diplomatic circles and in the O'Brien administration soared.

CHAPTER 6
AUTOPSY

The former President's body had been flown to Grand Rapids from Holland for the autopsy. Initial results were consistent with a heart attack.

But in keeping with Special Agent Bone's request, blood had been extracted for screening. Given the high profile of the victim - which Bone considered any deceased person to be if he was investigating the death - he also ordered an M.R.I to be run. This picked up evidence of physiological irregularities in the lower abdomen. They were slight enough to be an anomaly in the M.R.I. So Bone directed the M.R.I. be run again. They still showed up. Bone asked both radiologist and pathologist about the readings. They offered little insight.

"Could just be a quirk in the ex-President's neurological system," speculated the radiologist, flattered to be involved in the investigation of a deceased world leader; but revealing a physician's wariness at speculating on anything more.

"Could be. May be. That gets me no where" Bone growled. "We need facts and reliable explanations or we have nothing."

"Anything detected in the blood?" he barked.

The doctor, not used to being so bluntly challenged, reacted defensively.

"Well, we just extracted the blood a half hour ago. The lab will need to screen for abnormalities. That'll probably take at least two days."

"That's unacceptable" Bone barked. "We're dealing with the death of a former president and you're telling me that we have to wait two days for some lab tech to get around to completing tests? Light a fire! Or I'll do it – and you won't like the consequences if that happens."

Bone sometimes surprised even himself with his aggressive manner. Though intent on his work, he didn't particularly like lashing out at people the way he had now. Maybe it was the importance of the case. Maybe irritation with the doctor's bureaucratic attitude. Or maybe it was the fact his Sunday evening chicken dinner had been disrupted.

Then again, the explanation for his short fuse may have been credited at least in part to the fact the coroner had his radio tuned to Charlie Gasser's talk show. Gasser was in Bone's estimation a "blug" - someone his father once cryptically defined as "six pounds of shit in a five pound bag". Perpetually bemoaning the decaying state of American morals and regularly condemning illegal immigration, Gasser himself had been implicated in a sting operation involving child pornography and caught employing three undocumented workers as house servants several years earlier . Yet, amazingly, his listeners accepted his "heartfelt apology as a mortal sinner" and went right back to tuning in.

On this particular broadcast, Gasser's guest was Rod Churlish, a former National Security Advisor. Churlish had parlayed his lengthy government career into a lucrative career spent largely criticizing government and lobbying for large corporations. His views on the world, like those of nearly all of Gasser's guests, paralleled Gasser's own.

On this afternoon, the talk show host led off with:

"We got word tonight that ex-President Joshua Johnson died of an apparent heart attack while swimming off his lakeshore mansion in Michigan. Any thoughts on the passing of this infamous liberal?"

Geesh, Bone thought to himself, don't they even give a

respectful pause in criticizing someone when he cashes in his chips? But then he recalled the word "respectful" didn't find much space in some folk's vocabulary. Gasser was one of them.

"Well," Churlish replied with an affected drawl, "He wasn't one of my favorite ex-Presidents as your listeners know. I thought his work over the last eighteen months, pushing for global limits on economic growth in the name of the environment, was almost un-American. We can't tie our national economy or well-being to the wishes of a bunch of diplomats in the Hague or some other foreign place. And we sure as hell – pardon my French – shouldn't be submitting our authority over citizens and American businesses to some foreign judge or international authority sitting in some two-bit country an ocean away. That's what Johnson seemed to want and, in my humble opinion, he did America a great disservice."

Make that two people who don't know the meaning of the word "respectful", Bone thought. "Humble" wasn't a word he would associate with Rod Churlish. Churlish had always struck Bone as about as humble as a peacock in heat. Eager for war, Churlish had sought repeated deferments when he was of draft age. Resentful of government, he'd made his very comfortable living in government or attacking it.

Bone got the name of the lab where the blood work was being done and called the lab chief to push for immediate screening of Johnson's blood. He wasn't sure what he was looking for. But something other than the Lake Michigan shoreline smelled fishy to him. He instructed the lab chief to conduct a full blood profile – including a search for any unusual chemical, biological or other agents that could be traced. He also mentioned the M.R.I. and the electronic activity it picked up. The lab chief too seemed puzzled by the reading; but offered no new insights. He assured Bone he would run all the available tests to see what he could find.

Then he asked, almost as an afterthought: "Was the former President wearing any kind of electronic apparatus when he died?"

"Why'd you ask? " Bone pushed, the edge coming back into his voice.

"It's probably nothing", the lab chief responded. Bone's experience indicated these words usually meant just the opposite.

"It's just that I recently read an article in a trade journal, the <u>Journal of Professional Medical Examiners</u>, about a certain medical apparatus used to stimulate heart rates or other physiological functions which was supposedly being adapted by some scientists. The concern raised was that this device could potentially be reduced in size by new technology and then be planted in targets. It could then be remotely triggered to cause extreme results; things like a heart attack. Sort of like the Improvised Explosive Devices or IED's detonated along roadways during the Iraq and Afghan wars some years ago. Only here they'd be set to go off inside the body of a target. Scary thought, isn't it". He paused.

"But since the implant would require access to the body of a subject, the writer of the article concluded, it couldn't be much of a threat we need to be concerned about. An electronic device worn on the outside of the body would be easier to control and supposedly might be rigged to have the same result. But here, you say the pager fell off before the heart attack. Besides with a former president there would be the added protection of his Secret Service detail securing the areas around him. So it's probably not worth considering."

Bone listened attentively to the musings of the lab tech.

"Probably not", he muttered as he began to consider a new angle.

CHAPTER 7

THE SUMMIT

As the Somali crisis unfolded, another development with much broader implications was continuing to unfold globally. A series of crises, from Hurricane Katrina in 2007, to severe droughts and waves of tornadoes in the U.S., Africa, and Europe, and the emergence of new strains of tropical illnesses like malaria in traditionally temperate weather zones, were all spreading their deadly influence around the world. In some respects the leaders were followers in what evolved, as the general public began to "connect the dots" of the spiraling effects of climate change and challenged their elected or anointed leaders to do more.

As with many things, it began as a matter of economics. Five dollar a gallon gasoline in the U.S., food shortages and soaring consumer prices in Europe and Asia and costs of handling displaced refugees, touched nearly everyone. Insurance premiums soared in industrialized nations, especially in coastal regions, stifling development in regions occupied by a quarter of the world's population. The public's outrage finally fueled a political will to deal with the problem of climate change with heightened urgency.

Thus convened the First International Summit on Environmental Responsibility under the sponsorship of the United Nations. The Summit was unique in that it was truly global – with developed, developing and underdeveloped countries all represented at the table. The fact it was defined as the "first annual" Summit, acknowledged not only the nature of the conference but the intention that this mark the beginning of an ongoing process of intensified global environmentalism.

Into this mix, President Johnson found himself thrust in a leading role following his creative involvement in Mideast peace negotiations and the more recent Somali crisis. Over the considerable protest of key advisors, President O'Brien appointed Johnson as his special envoy to the gathering. The two Presidents had developed a curiously close, if guarded, working relationship through the Somali incident. In a phenomenon little remarked but frequently occurring in politics, two coming from contrasting backgrounds, constituencies, and orientations had developed a mutual respect that seemed only to deepen through awareness of their differences and curiosity to understand the other better. The fact close friends privately called them the "Odd Couple" didn't seem to dissuade either of these independent-minded formal rivals from building a relationship of growing trust. It didn't hurt that Johnson had made clear his career in elective politics was at an end and that the role of "ambassador at large" on a range of global issues suited him entirely.

Now the pattern set in Somalia was followed by the current President giving his predecessor broad latitude to follow in the negotiation process. Of course, Secretary of State Michaud was to head the official delegation. But she understood the key role the former President was to play based on a candid visit with her boss.

The Conference convened with the following broad objectives:

1. To establish a consensus on the magnitude of environmental crises, both as to scope and severity;

2. To reach agreement on primary causes of the crisis;

whether greenhouse gases, resource depletion, or other conditions;

3. To define tangible and measurable goals for addressing these causes; and finally,

4. To develop a model for developed and developing countries to pursue in meeting their respective goals and outcomes.

Such broad and comprehensive goals fueled high expectations likely to be disappointed. But a couple of recent major catastrophes - one in the U.S. and one in China - had roused the anxiety of these two powerful nations with demands for action now. First, in the U.S. a highly resistant strain of malaria had surfaced that resulted in the agonizing deaths of over fifteen thousand people in a half dozen cities. Troubling though this was in its own right, the epidemic had occurred in the upper Midwest – an area never even associated with this historically tropical disease. Through intense research efforts, a vaccine had finally been developed. But only after frightening damage from the warming climate had already been done.

Then, within six months of this malaria outbreak, in Beijing, China, the profound air pollution caused by China's rapid industrialization resulted in a wave of deaths from pulmonary edema and embolisms. Among the victims was the adored oldest son of the Chinese Premier. The mourning of the supreme leader of China had been public and profound.

Because of Johnson's success in crafting an environmentally creative solution to the thorny problem in Somalia, the former President had been asked to give the keynote address to the conference.

Never the most eloquent orator, Johnson's power as a speaker came from the intensity and sincerity with which he spoke, as well as an earnest desire to lend value to whatever the topic or audience he was addressing.

As he considered his comments for the Summit, he felt a burden greater than any he'd experienced before in public life. Never had so much seemed to hang in the balance for the future of life on this planet. And never were expectations so high.

The result of his struggle was both memorable and moving.

He began his remarks by placing the global environmental crises in the context of human history.

"Our human species has, from ancient times, considered itself in many cultural traditions as the crowning glory of nature. Fueled with religious teachings that make us masters of our world - fed by our own ability to bind and control nature to meet our ever expanding needs - we have often seen ourselves as less part of nature than as superior to it. If droughts seem likely, we build bigger barns to store more grain during times of plenty. If blight kills crops or livestock, we create hybrids or develop vaccines to reverse nature's order. As our population expands, we've come up with ways to vastly increase crop yields to meet our mounting needs. We've even seeded rain clouds to bring rain; and leveed or dammed our rivers and streams to tame their wilder seasons.

"Through it all, we have acted on the assumption that human life is of transcendent importance and that nature exists largely for humanity's fulfillment and well being.

"We are, in truth, a remarkable species. We have grown from a couple thousand huddled ancestors seventy thousand years ago, to well over seven billion people today. And over the last two hundred years, our species has shaped, corralled, and disciplined nature like no other species our planet has ever seen.

"Yet, we are still a part of nature, as dependent as any other species on its providence and well being. We may bridle the oceans with dykes or levees, yet Force Five hurricanes will still overwhelm them. We may bioengineer bountiful crops to resist disease. But in the process, we encourage ever more resistant beetles, weevils, and viruses to attack them. We may foster better medicines and procedures to prolong human life. But in the process we create shortages and depletion of resources for future generations.

"Our faith teaches us that, in the words of Genesis, although we may have the power to subdue the Earth and have dominion over it, (Genesis 1:28); we are also called upon to replenish it and to be good stewards of our natural bounty. For, as the Koran reminds us, the Earth is the Lord's and not truly our own (Koran, Sura 22:64-66)."

"It is our duty in these challenging times to recognize forthrightly that humanity, though remarkable in every sense of the word, is still a part of nature, dependent on natural law like all other species. If we break nature's laws, or abuse them, nature will deal with our species as it has with others before us, and we will be decimated.

"Ours then is the singular task at this end of history to bring our customs and habits in line with practices that are sustainable over time. It is our task to develop customs that will not cheat our children, grandchildren and posterity, out of their right to thrive in the future.

"The great American President, Abraham Lincoln, spoke words in his second annual message to Congress that ring true to us gathered here today: He said, 'The dogmas of the quiet past are unequal to the stormy present. The occasion is piled high with difficulty and we must rise to the occasion... We cannot escape history. We will be remembered in spite of ourselves. No personal significance or insignificance can spare one or another of us. The fiery trial through which we pass will light us down in honor or dishonor to the latest generation'.

"In this conference and those to follow, may we be as creative and as supple in our thinking, as generous to the future, and as honest with ourselves, as the best of human nature allows us to be. May we identify new ways of life <u>less</u> concerned with indiscriminate consumption and <u>more</u> with conservation. Yes, may we be <u>conservative</u> in the oldest and best sense of the word ...acting as good stewards to <u>conserve</u> the bounty with which we have been blessed. May we create mechanisms that cause us to consume less, conserve more, and live within sustainable customs.

"Then in Lincoln's words, will our names be written down in honor, not dishonor, to the latest generation."

Then, the former president sat down.

The audience paused when Johnson finished – startled at the brevity and directness of his challenge. Then, to a person, they rose to their feet and applauded.

The tone was set. The gauntlet tossed. And those attending the conference felt emboldened to tackle the vast challenge at hand.

CHAPTER 8
RESULTS

It took twenty-four hours to get the lab results back on the late President's blood work. No evidence of any kind of toxicity was detected and the official results were all negative of any pathological problems.

The medical lab chief's remarks, had in the meantime, prompted Bone to get on the Internet and download the article from the Journal of Professional Medical Examiners which had been mentioned. Its contents were consistent with what Bone had been told, though one comment in particular caught his eye. The author, largely speculating on the point, suggested:

"It may well be assumed that clandestine organizations may explore ways to utilize these sophisticated internal electronic devices. This will doubtless prompt intelligence communities and nations that could be targeted to prepare suitable methods of response."

The writer of the article was a Dr. Hassim Nakob who had formerly worked for the Egyptian Intelligence Service before immigrating to the U.S. following the overthrow of long-time Egyptian strongman, Hosni Mubarek in 2011. Nakob had maintained contact with the agency where he formerly worked, thus gaining access to certain underground circles in the Middle East.

For security reasons, Bone set up an appointment with Dr. Nakob at his office in New York City that afternoon. Nakob was remote, no doubt alarmed by Bone's disclosure he was with the F.B.I.

Bone got straight to the point.

"Doctor I read your article on electronic implants from the Journal of Professional Medical Examiners and need to ask you some questions".

"May I ask what this is concerning" the Doctor asked guardedly.

"Afraid not. Let's just say it's for background on an investigation we are in the middle of".

Not waiting for a response, Bone plowed forward.

"How far advanced is this technology."

"I'm not sure I understand your question. But the concept really just incorporates existing mechanisms in new, though I may say, pretty diabolical ways. The new dimension is to do things with such small microchips as to be able to be almost undetectable. The object implanted could potentially be almost microscopic in size. Something that could be ingested without the subject even being aware of it."

"By eating?" Bone asked.

"Yes, of course" the Doctor replied matter of factly. "Then the device could be triggered remotely to create abnormalities that would prove fatal to the victim".

"I see" Bone pondered considering this new possibility. "Who's pursuing this?" He didn't ask if a heart attack was one possible consequence, to shield the reason for his questioning.

"Again, I really cannot say. But I expect any number of groups – including some legitimate government organizations in this country, of course, to head off hostile acts by terrorist organizations through countermeasures".

Bone let slide the obvious question triggered by this last remark. Doctor Nakob, a foreign national, affiliated with a private university would not seem to have legitimate access to any classified information. However Bone knew enough about the intelligence community to know that matters passed in and out of authorized channels, which could lead to an unauthorized but well placed individuals gaining information on emerging technologies of even the most sensitive nature.

"How far away from implementation would this technology be?"

Dr. Nakob responded, "My sources, you will understand, must remain strictly confidential or lives would be in danger." He paused, "However, I have been led to believe these devices may be available as we speak."

Admonishing the doctor of the strict confidentiality of their visit, Bone flew back to Grand Rapids that same night. He returned to Friendship Heights to review the site again. The former President's routine had been to leave his cabin at 7:00 p.m.; walk directly to the pier below the cabin and then wade into the lake until he was up to his waist. Then he vigorously pushed off in a crawl stroke with which he'd swim to a point a half mile out in the lake. A buoy had been placed at the turnaround point which he would customarily circle, and then swim directly back to shore. The Secret Service boat would be kept at a 25 yard distance – down- wind to avoid the fumes – and track the President's progress out and back. The only thing that could disrupt the routine would be if Johnson got an urgent message on his pager – a number very narrowly circulated to certain heads of state, and his trusted assistant, Lydia Stonecraft. Dr. Stonecraft knew, however, not to bother him while he was swimming except in the most dire emergency.

In short, he was accessible, but only to a very few and almost never while he was swimming.

The pager itself reflected no message for the last 15 minutes before his 7:00 cabin departure. The device was attached by a Velcro-edged pouch to a nylon belt Johnson wore while swimming. The belt apparatus appeared to be in order, except for the small pouch holding the pager, which somehow had separated from the nylon belt, thus accounting for the pager falling off as the President waded into the lake. Inspection had revealed the glue by which the pouch was attached to the belt had given way causing the separation. Innocent enough on its face, Bone thought; though the timing seemed suspicious enough he'd ordered a chemical analysis of the pouch and the belt itself.

Fingerprint scans on the pager turned up nothing other than compromised prints of the former President. Prior messages revealed a call from Dr. Stonecraft earlier in the afternoon, which Secret Service Agent Le Beau indicated the President had answered. Bone contacted the scientist to see what the conversation concerned.

His call found her bereft. Given his nature and stage of the investigation, naturally Bone pushed forward anyway.

"Dr. Stonecraft, I understand your loss at the death of President Johnson. But I need to ask you about events leading up to his death at Friendship Point".

She seemed oddly comforted that inquiries were being made by the F.B.I.

"I'll try to help; though it just doesn't seem real that he's gone. He was so full of life and ...well, physically vigorous until the moment of his death" she reflected.

"That's partly why we are looking into this. Can you tell me what the two of you talked about the afternoon before he died?"

"Well, a lot of things we usually discussed. How progress was going with getting the goals of the global summit clarified and agreed upon. How work on adoption of the <u>Template</u> was progressing ..."

"Tell me about that. I've heard reference in the press to the <u>Template</u>. But, I'll be frank with you, I hadn't paid a whole lot of attention until the President's death".

"You should have" she responded earnestly. "It was a set of standards President Johnson crafted to reshape the way we deal with the environment of the world around us – from man-made to natural habitats."

"Pretty controversial stuff, I suppose," Agent Bone prompted.

"Of course. There was enormous opposition at first. From OPEC to car manufacturers, to big retailers who saw the <u>Template</u> undercutting their whole way of doing business." She paused.

"But in spite of that, it seemed to be catching on. People seemed to be getting it; that we <u>do</u> have to change the way we live if we want to go on living on our planet with any semblance of the quality of life we've known for our children. The support of Saudi Arabia and Syria, as well as other Arab countries for the deal Joshua worked out in Somalia evidenced how opponents could be brought on board, even though that deal was based on using alternative non-fossil fuels." She paused again.

Bone was interested but focused on his investigation. "So any one in particular you think of who didn't 'get it' as you put it; who would want to harm the former President?"

"I'm sure there are a lot of people like that out there. But right now I'm having a hard time getting my brain around Joshua's being gone, much less who could have had a motive in making it happen. I'm sorry." She started to cry.

Bone tried to wrap things up. "I understand Doctor. Thanks for talking. I may be back in touch. In the meantime, if you think of anything else or need to talk, call me." He gave her his cell phone number. It was his turn to pause. Something inside prompted him to add, "And again I'm very sorry for your loss."

"The whole world will be sorry," she sighed softly as she hung up.

The lab results on the examination of the belt arrived later that evening. Traces of a chemical associated with glue solvent were detected on the belt - a chemical that was water activated.

CHAPTER 9
THE TEMPLATE

The First International Summit on Environmental Responsibility, to nearly everyone's surprise, had made remarkable progress in realizing the ambitious goals it set for itself. Consensus was reached on the magnitude of the problem and key contributing factors. Among those issues prompting considerable debate was the effect of surging global population, projected to grow to over nine billion people by the year 2040. Issues regarding population control, including traditional methods of abstinence and contraception as well as abortion, were heatedly argued. The Vatican, represented by a special Legate, had initially resisted any declaration advocating anything other than abstinence.

But, in a remarkable reconsideration of church doctrine midway through the conference, the Legate announced revision of opposition to scientific methods of contraception. The Pope himself modified the earlier Encyclical "Humanae Vitae" to address the impact on human life as well as the natural world, of human population continuing to expand at accelerating rates. In a particularly poignant passage, the Pope wrote:

"We have become increasingly mindful of the truth that humanity, though created in the image of God, is nevertheless dependent upon and a part of the natural world which God also created. This natural world is itself subject to changeable but still finite limits.

"We must therefore consider the quality as well as the

quantity of human life, as one directly impacts upon the other. If this is not considered, the process of preserving or prolonging human life may, in the long term, actually endanger human survival, through environmental depletion and the natural disasters it brings. Drought, famine, warfare, and genocide can and already have followed from these changes to our environment.

"As stewards of the environment and as children of God, we have given acute and intense moral consideration to the deadly effects of swelling global population. This consideration has led us to favor medically proven and safe methods which prevent unintended conceptions; as distinguished from those procedures which terminate life already conceived which we continue to oppose and condemn as offending what is sacred.

"Similarly, at the end of mortal life, measures which artificially prolong life, against a person's wishes and desire that life end naturally, must be reconsidered as to the moral as well as medical ethics of such measures."

This declaration had profound impact on the dialogue at the summit and helped break the impasse over the subject of population control as an element of dealing with environmental crises. Excessive consumption and shortages could only grow more pronounced if human population continued to grow unchecked.

Then former President Johnson followed his keynote address by submitting a series of principles which he entitled "A Template for our Times". His remarks to the plenary session of the Conference, began with the following introduction:

"Our world represents a remarkable synthesis of conflicting forces that have come   together to create a place where life can survive and thrive. The balance of energy and matter; the complementary quality of plant and animal life;

the adaptive qualities of our natural environment to absorb and compensate for change; have all allowed the human race to emerge and to prosper on this small, green planet in the cosmos.

"Now we are confronted by the consequences of our own success. Able to adapt to changing circumstances, we have found cures for once fatal illnesses, developed inventions to turn the night into day, and tools to ward off winter's cold and summer's heat. We have tamed nature to conform it to our needs and – in more recent centuries – to our desires and whims.

"Our environment has never experienced anything quite like the human race. Any other species that multiplied at the rate ours does, or consumed resources with the voracious appetite ours displays, would quickly overwhelm the system and die off - in large part by famine or disease. Any hunter or fisherman knows the consequences of a species, deprived of natural predators, overpopulating a forest or stream: it soon faces depletion of needed resources and mass starvation.

"Yet we humans have survived the bubonic plague, countless famines, and even our own propensity for killing off each other with ever more ingenious weapons of destruction in that unique human ritual called war. We have seemingly come back from each of these natural and manmade disasters stronger – or at least more numerous – than ever.

"But despite our ingenuity and creative powers, we still live within the confines of a natural world that imposes its own immutable laws and limits. We cannot live without oxygen, food and water. If any one of these is cut off, human life – not to mention much of the other life on this planet – comes to an end. Plants may seem the humblest and most passive of all creatures. Yet without the life-giving oxygen they produce in exchange for the carbon dioxide they absorb, virtually all animal life would perish. Energy and matter are forever changing places – as wood is converted by fire to heat and light, and the energy of sunlight is converted by plants to the matter cellulose. Meanwhile, some forms of matter – for example, wood or coal – are more easily converted to useful energy than other forms – say, our garbage or other waste streams.

"We humans tend to regard the world as our personal property to use or squander as we see fit; and often seem to believe any problems can be solved with our inimitable minds and engineering skills. To be sure, these minds, particularly tempered by an understanding spirit, can solve much – probably even the problems of the much misused environment around us today.

"But we do well to remember that, whatever our gifts, we are still subject to natural laws of demand and depletion.

"My proposal sets out in broad terms, a <u>Template</u> to help assure our response to the challenges and opportunities our overpopulated, overextended planet faces will be that of a good steward, husbanding our planet for the benefit of future generations."

Then former President Johnson concluded:

"This response will involve changing the way we approach nature and one another. As wiser minds have suggested before, how we treat the environment is ultimately a direct corollary of how we treat each other. As poet-conservationist, Wendell Berry once noted: 'The earth is what we all have in common. There is an uncanny resemblance between our behavior towards each other and our behavior towards the earth. By some connection, we do not recognize the willingness to exploit one becomes the willingness to exploit the other...it is impossible to care for each other more or differently than we care for the Earth'".

Then Johnson's <u>Template</u> identified four simple yet exacting tests for evaluating the environmental impact and value of any new product or process. In a working draft he presented to the Conference the four tests were outlined as follows:

"1. <u>Is it necessary?</u> This simple question is loaded with problems. What one person - say, a socialite in a developed county who is accustomed to lavish parties and lifestyle - considers necessary is significantly different from that of a monk living in isolation in a cell in Italy or Thailand. One may therefore argue the question is meaningless. But that is a cop out. For even with the vast diversity of definitions of necessity, there are still certain realities that influence us all and define our basic needs. Food, clothing, shelter, and reasonable security from arbitrary loss of these things gives us a starting point. In the United States, our founders defined basic necessities in terms of life, liberty and the pursuit of happiness.

"A moral society should seek to provide a reasonable opportunity to meet the basic needs for all its citizens. The citizens themselves have a duty to embrace that opportunity and behave so as not to forfeit those rights, by breaking laws; or jeopardize other people's rights to experience them, by exploiting the disadvantaged or behaving irresponsibly. As it relates to the environment, the question of 'is it necessary'? forces us to look more critically at what we choose to do or to consume. It calls upon a higher level of consciousness to seriously consider our alternatives in cutting back or eliminating unnecessary things, thereby reducing the useless consumption that depletes resources needed for our future generations.

"For those faced daily with issues of survival, the question in its own cruel way, may be easiest: the choice of luxuries or indulgent lives is simply not there. For those of us living in more prosperous countries, where it's commonplace to indulge in what much of the world would consider to be luxuries, this test becomes more sacrificial and deliberate. Do we need the gas guzzling SUV or the latest flat screen television if the car or television we already have works perfectly well? Do we need 3,000 square feet of housing for empty nesters, or a second house for two months vacation each winter? Do we need to bag our groceries in plastic instead of using recyclable canvas? Do we need to buy water in a plastic bottle with a fancy label, when tap water drawn into a recyclable glass does just as well?

"'Need' is an expansive term. But common sense provides some practical limits on how we define it. We must all try harder to apply it to our daily choices.

> "2. <u>Does it conserve?</u> As the question 'is it necessary', causes us to consider lifestyle choices, the second test points us towards products or processes that minimize use of materials. Conservation has a long political history. As early as 1900, Theodore Roosevelt was championing an approach to the environment that saw husbanding or caring for nature as part of our duty to future generations. 'Conserve' is, after all, the root word for the label 'conservative', which not only applies to a cautious approach

to social change, but a desire to preserve what we have and not to unduly jeopardize it.

"In evaluating whether something conserves, we may ask whether the method of growing crops minimizes waste of top soil; or a system for heating our houses minimizes energy loss. We may consider how to move more people or products to where they need to go with less energy; for, example by, passenger or freight rail service instead of personal automobiles. Or we may consider whether a process for disseminating information cuts waste paper, labor or energy.

"Technology affords marvelous opportunities for conserving resources. Dissemination of information on the Internet is one example. Using pure energy sources – wind, water, and solar –offer an increasingly viable alternative to fossil fuels that are more environmentally friendly and help conserve natural wilderness areas.

"By applying the second test, we come closer to realizing the conservative ideal of preserving what we have been entrusted for the benefit and enjoyment of all future generations.

"3. <u>Does it reduce or eliminate waste and is the remaining waste stream manageable?</u> This critical test gets to the heart of the environmental crisis with which we are faced today. For the whole issue of global warming is the direct result of producing more waste – specifically CO_2 and other greenhouse gases – than the environment can naturally absorb.

"The first two tests - considering what is necessary and what conserves - both point to this third test: reducing waste.

If we are to survive and thrive as a species, we need to get a handle on this problem.

"Simply put, we can reduce our waste stream or it will reduce us – socially, economically, and politically. The pollution we cause contaminates our water, fouls the air we breathe, and melts polar ice to cause vast population displacements.

"Processes or products that produce little waste, for example, the pure energy sources of wind, sun and water, can all go far in meeting this test. Nuclear power, at least from nuclear fission, provides a potentially vast source of available power. Regrettably, it also produces a waste stream that is neither harmless nor particularly manageable, unless we can come up with a way to shorten the half life of spent nuclear fuel. The proliferation of nuclear power facilities in countries which also covet nuclear weapons merely underscores another problem with this tempting but troublesome energy source.

"Ideally, we should be striving for a <u>waste free</u> civilization. In such a civilization every waste product of human activity could be reutilized or recycled in some new usable product. Much of the technology exists for this already - from strippable newsprint, to glass houses made from broken bottles, to athletic fields and tracks made from recycled tires. To the extent this ideal cannot be met and waste is left over, we should seek to assure that the types of waste will not be such as to bedevil the future with consequences like global warming or nuclear meltdowns.

"4. <u>Is it sustainable?</u> This fourth and final test, which involves a watchword of 21ˢᵗ Century environmentalism, considers whether a product or process can be indefinitely maintained over time. It may rely on virtually infinite resources – like sun and wind – or merely on resources that can be regrown or regenerated fairly quickly – like bamboo as a building material.

"The sustainability of a product or process is critical to avoid depletion of natural resources, which, when spent, are essentially gone forever. It took millions of years of intense pressure and heat below the surface of the Earth to produce fossil fuels. When used up, they cannot be reasonably restored for a similar period of time.

"Sustainability also focuses on the <u>impact</u> of resources used. A truly sustainable product or process should leave a minimal footprint for the future to worry about. Something which is limitless, but leaves dire, irresolvable problems for those who came after, is not truly sustainable. The consequences to the future will be to significantly diminish the lives of those who inherit our mistakes."

* * *

The <u>Template for Our Time</u> then concluded with a proposal for adopting the <u>Template</u> as a four part rating system that would assign points or credits to every new product or process based on each of the four <u>Template</u> tests. The higher the point total, the better the product from an environmental perspective.

As with other declarations that challenge long held beliefs, Johnson's <u>Template</u> inspired both thoughtful comment and hostile condemnation. Some economists in attendance argued that the <u>Template</u>, if adopted, could stifle economic productivity and growth. They pointed out that all market-based economic systems depend upon consumption – not conservation – and that any regulatory scheme enforcing the <u>Template</u> could kill off growth. Some government leaders argued the <u>Template</u> could impair not only economic growth and prosperity, but the natural human impulse for self-improvement - allowing one to be rewarded for one's efforts. And leaders of developing countries argued the <u>Template</u> could freeze them in a state of impoverishment by tying their hands from exploiting the environment the way developed countries had already done over the prior two centuries.

To these objections, President Johnson led a consortium of economists and biologists which Dr. Stonecraft had helped assemble. They demonstrated point by point that adopting the <u>Template</u> would not result in economic slowdown since it would prompt a whole new raft of industries based on principles of conservation and sustainability. Purchase and consumption of re-structured products and processes would actually boost economic expansion. Developing countries would benefit doubly by both experiencing sustainable development in line with emerging rather than obsolete technology, and by conserving vital resources like rain forests that might otherwise have been destroyed.

What Johnson came to realize was that the real challenge was getting people to think beyond themselves and into the future for their children. Left to our natural instincts he reflected, we protect what gives us comfort or has worked for us in the past. The hope now lay in appealing both to our moral sense of responsibility to one another and broader concerns for the well-being of our own children and grandchildren.

But the "bird in the hand" backlash pushed back: better to have the comforts we know now even though they may bring problems later, than to lose them for some possible future benefit which may or may not happen. Such selfish and short-sighted thinking, Johnson reflected, was as natural as breathing and about as hard to change.

Something was needed to "shift the paradigm". The Vatican's pronouncement recognizing the moral imperatives caused by over-population helped. But an almost freakish series of global incidents occurred, beginning midway through the Conference.

First, came another outbreak of malaria, this time in Central Germany – again in a climate never associated with malaria before.

Then, in Indonesia and India, record breaking tsunamis struck coastal areas killing tens of thousands in both countries. Tsunami detection systems had failed to alert coastal regions due to the short circuiting of the devices because of anomalies in magnetic fields as a result of atmospheric changes.

Finally, the City of New York experienced a rolling black-out over three days as the energy grid shut down amidst a heat wave sweeping the Northeastern U.S.

Some remarked the series of natural disasters seemed almost Biblical in nature – like the plagues affecting Egypt in the book of Exodus. Only here they came as a warning from the Creator that greater care of his creation was urgently needed. Others, huddled in darkened meeting halls at the U.N., drew less theological but no less urgent conclusions from the disasters.

Recalling the observation by the English writer Samuel Johnson that "it is remarkable what an appointment with the gallows a fortnight hence will do to focus the concentration", the Secretary General of the U.N. urged the Summit to immediate action. In a remarkable show of unity, the assembled delegates with few dissenting votes, endorsed the recommendations of the Steering Committee and adopted Johnson's Template for Our Time, as the standard by which new products or processes should be measured on a global basis.

CHAPTER 10
CONSEQUENCES

Despite the mounting climate disasters, and results of the First Annual Summit in adopting the Template, interest groups lobbying against it were well organized to obstruct its legislative approval in many nations.

Yet as its adoption soaked in, the reaction of industries, including utilities and equipment manufacturers, astonished many-including politicians from nations where these industries were based. For the magnitude of the climate change problems had roused a consciousness perhaps unlike anything since the U.S. reaction to Pearl Harbor in 1941. In this instance, however, the consciousness was global and collaborative and not adversarial between nations.

To be sure, there were conflicting national interests involved. But now global competition shifted from merely producing more, to seeking to surpass one another in developing more cost effective hydrogen cells or solar batteries; or in multiplying the percentage of a nation's population employed in green industries.

A new consciousness began to pervade global politics. It was at once concerned and cooperative. A consciousness returned to one last seen when the first astronaut stepped on the moon in 1969 and, with cameras beaming back to Earth, humanity first saw ours as a beautiful but vulnerable blue-green sphere in the vastness of space. Globally, people again spoke of our planet as "Spaceship Earth". Individually and by nation, humankind gradually began to see that the real threat that confronted us did not come from some alien power but from our own bad habits. Like a recovering alcoholic, people still possessed a strong impulse towards consumption. But they came to see these impulses as being hurtful to loved ones, and thus conduct to be avoided or at least restrained.

Yet, some businesses had so invested themselves in traditional fossil fuels they could see no way to convert. They fought the rising tide of change by lobbying against the Template and appealing to fear. Layoffs; rising costs of fuel or food; and loss of quality of life were all cited as the inevitable consequences of the Template, despite mounting evidence to the contrary. Meanwhile, others, out of conviction or convenience, invoked greed as a reason to avoid the Template. These individuals maintained the new world order would stifle national identities in a wave of global standards. They complained that the Template would "prevent us from enjoying the full range of choice" the old system afforded. The underlying irony of these arguments – that unborn future generations could well lack any meaningful range of choice – was ignored.

Over succeeding months, this last group became the most strident. They disrupted town hall meetings, orchestrated letters to the editor campaigns in vulnerable elected officials' districts, and weighed in daily during radio broadcasts condemning the Template.

But despite these invectives, the tide was turning. People battered by savage storms, or facing drought and other environmental disasters, were ready to change. As more than one commentator remarked "that train has left the station".

New Green initiatives were announced almost daily. 'Feed in' rates guaranteeing customers-installed solar systems favorable rates for up to twenty years, were adopted in England. Tax credits favoring investment in alternate energy for up to 15 year were adopted in the U.S. And new Personal

Sustainability Devices, or "P.S.D.'s" – powered by human body heat or motion - began filling the marketplace.

"Green" became the new gold standard. Industries and nations were vying with each other to innovate new conservation, recycling, and sustainable processes to earn higher Template ratings.

And Joshua Johnson was at the center of the initiatives in promoting change.

CHAPTER 11
SUSPECTS

When special agent Bone received the lab results showing chemical traces on the President's swimming belt, his brain shifted to overdrive. His first concern was to determine who knew of the lab results and then to keep the circle closed. He'd ordered the tests done without the knowledge of the Secret Service, after retrieving the belt and pager for his investigation

Bone had known Monty Le Beau for over 30 years. They had served in the Marines in the first Persian Gulf War and went through F.B.I. training together afterwards. Le Beau was recruited for the Secret Service because of his special forces training in the Marines, and because his deliberate yet daring manner appealed to the Service chief. Derrick and Le Beau had been personal friends as well, and Le Beau had even accompanied Bone on fishing trips on Lake Michigan when their schedules allowed.

Yet in the investigation, Bone didn't even feel comfortable talking to his old friend about his growing suspicions. He requisitioned records on all contacts the President had made the week before his death and, as the former President had been fairly compulsive, these records were lengthy.

Within the preceding week, the ex-President had: (1) been approached by ten national and international radio and television talk shows about doing guest appearances to discuss the Template and how it would affect their audiences; (2) visited with three heads of state concerning procedural issues in timing <u>Template</u> adoption within their countries; and (3) visited with six union leaders who warned Johnson about the political problems caused by promoting a strong environmental agenda. These were just the messages that survived Laura Stonecraft's screening process, which aimed to cut away all contacts beyond what she knew from years of experience the former President would want to review.

Nothing jumped out at Bone. All predictable contacts; all entirely expected concerns. He looked further. Very discreetly he obtained phone logs of Johnson's Secret Service detail. These included calls made to check with local law enforcement about security measures for the ex-President's movement within the Southwest Michigan area and communications regarding a forthcoming trip to the European Union Johnson was to make next month to bolster support for the <u>Template</u> rating system.

Of greatest interest, Bone reviewed Secret Service communications including threats made on the ex-President's life. These included the usual "hate mail" saying Joshua Johnson deserved to roast in hell for what he'd done to change our way of life; or comparing him to Hitler.

But there were two that caught his eye. One concerned a threat – Mideast in origin – by certain Muslim extremists issued against the "infidel" undermining Islamic power by encouraging a radical shift away from fossil fuels. The other was an incoming e-mail from Rod Churlish, the former NSA Chief, to Dick Rodman. The message was simply "the package has arrived". There was no recorded response from Rodman.

CHAPTER 12

ENCIRCLEMENT

Special Agent Bone had been working non-stop since he had gotten the call from the Chief two days before. With little more than naps snatched at odd moments between calls, he badly needed a good night's sleep.

Finally, the Chief ordered him home. He got there after 11:00 p.m. on Tuesday. As he let himself in, he noticed a slip of paper on the floor under his front door. It was an amateurish thing he knew, but a precaution obsessively followed anyways: wedging a slip of paper between his door and the frame whenever he left home to tell whether anyone had entered while he was gone. He did the same with the rear door and the door to the garage. Just as reflexively he'd check all slips when he got home.

When he saw the slip of paper on the floor, his drowsiness disappeared. He began a systematic survey of his house. Working for the Bureau had its advantages. He had electronic sweep equipment to search for bugs or other surveillance devices. He found two, a small receiver mounted in his bedroom study and another on the phone line entering the house to which his computer was linked. His mind again raced. He was unconcerned about the results of his investigation being compromised by these devices since he hadn't been home in two days. But what other surveillance was being conducted and by whom? He left the devices in place, since disconnecting them would only alert whoever was watching him. He decided to go a step further and feed a few false leads of his own. He sent a loosely encrypted message to the Chief reporting good progress in the investigation, and a forthcoming unremarkable conclusion. Then he swept his car for bugs. The result was negative.

But he was being watched, and he knew his cell phone would be monitored. For this reason, he had a backup phone in the spare tire compartment of his car. He would use this for the duration, and simply use his primary cell phone to place a few more leads to send whoever was tracing him on a wild goose chase or two.

In the meantime, he did a data search of the origins of the bugs in his house and found a trace to a private security firm in Grand Rapids with which he had done a fair amount of business. It would be easy enough to requisition records as part of a criminal investigation; but this would tip off whoever was following him that he was returning the favor.

Instead, he contacted a sales representative of the firm with whom he had an occasional drink. He asked him about equipment similar to the bugs placed in his house, inquiring generally of any recent purchases of the system, so he could see how well customers had been satisfied. The salesman, always eager to curry favor with an F.B.I. Agent, was more than happy to oblige despite the late hour.

Derrick scoured the list for familiar names. No individual names jumped out at him, but an institutional customer did: the U.S. Secret Service. A day earlier, the Secret Service had purchased identical surveillance equipment to that found in his house.

Bone turned over in his mind the Secret Service Agents on duty during the twelve hours preceding the President's death. He checked them off, one by one, for a variety of reasons; from inaccessibility to background. He was finally left with only two: his old friend, Monty Le Beau, and Dick

Rodman. Le Beau had the accessibility – he was in closer proximity to President Johnson than anyone else for several hours before his death. Bone also knew him to harbor pretty conservative political views that would, in all probability, not be in line with what the former President was attempting to accomplish globally.

But Bone had known Le Beau since the early '90's and knew his old friend had an ingrained respect for civilian authority extending back to his military service. Le Beau considered the Secret Service to be simply an extension of that. "Love 'em or hate 'em", he used to say, "If the people choose 'em, we stand up and salute and lay down our lives to keep 'em safe."

But, Bone considered, President Johnson had not been <u>elected</u> to his present mission. He'd been deputized by the current President and then expanded this to his world leadership role. Would the distinction have pushed Johnson out of the safety zone as far as Le Beau was concerned?

And what about Agent Rodman? He seemed defensive and tense that first night. But then, who wouldn't be if it was suggested that the President had died on his watch? Rodman too had rightward leanings. A search of his personnel file revealed he had associated with a number of right wing organizations over the years. His file also revealed that he had requested assignment to protect Rod Churlish when, as National Security Advisor, Churlish had made some inflammatory statements about Islam that triggered a flurry of death threats. The request had been granted and for the next six months, Rodman had been assigned to the security detail for Churlish.

Then there was that cryptic unanswered e-mail from Churlish.

Bone went back to his sales friend and asked if he had

met the guy who made the purchase for the Secret Service. He answered, "Sure, it was my sale."

"Do you remember his name?"

"Let's see. The guy was kind of evasive about giving a name", the salesman pondered. "But he got a call on his cell phone while he was with me. As I recall he answered, 'Rodman, here'."

CHAPTER 13

TRANSFORMATION

As the world moved, haltingly at first, then with growing momentum towards more environmentally responsible policies, nature continued to provide reminders of the urgent need for change. Rising tides in coastal regions required evacuation of portions of coastal cities - from Seattle, Washington to Portland, Maine to Sydney, Australia. Some cities like Hong Kong and Amsterdam, that had been hit by seemingly freak hurricanes; began to rebuild but further inland and with depleted populations.

As often happens when disaster strikes, people reacted in two principal ways. There were those who turned bitter over the experience and reacted first by denial and by then seeking to blame others for the devastation. Others, equally in denial at first, became engaged and determined to mitigate the problems.

In what seemed an affirmation of human decency, the second group greatly outnumbered the first. People pulled together against what seemed a common foe: humanity's own past carelessness.

Global initiatives increased. Information sharing on weather systems and storm monitoring became routine, even between traditional regional rivals like India and Pakistan or Israel and Syria. Mutual aid missions to respond to the growing crisis gave the militaries of nations around the World a massive and peaceful reuse of their logistical talents and resources.

In short, the Earth began to function more like a very large spaceship on which the occupant/astronauts realized they depended on each other for their collective survival.

In this context, word of the former President's death triggered a global reaction. From live broadcasts on the evening news to headlines and newspapers around the globe, a flood of comment – both pro and con – ricocheted around the world within hours of Johnson's death. Expressions of sadness came from all corners of the globe.

The reaction to the death was enhanced by the close association Johnson's <u>Template</u> had with the way the world was changing. He was seen as the architect and advocate for a new order that afforded hope, civility, and a new code of personal responsibility to unify the scattered peoples of the Earth. His death came like that of a respected patriarch, esteemed and beloved however remote. While economic and political resentments lingered towards the U.S. and its allies in underdeveloped parts of the world, Joshua Johnson had transcended national identity and come to be seen as a truly global leader – one concerned with social justice and the well being of future generations regardless of where they lived.

Heads of state expressed desire to attend what had initially been planned as a small and modest family funeral. That prompted the O'Brien Administration and Congress to declare a week of mourning commencing with a State Funeral at the National Cathedral in Washington. Johnson, a Lutheran by upbringing but with a decidedly ecumenical perspective towards each of the world's religions, would be honored with a memorial service in which clergy from Protestant, Roman Catholic, Greek Orthodoxy, Jewish, Muslim, Hindu, and Buddhist, as well as Native American holy men would participate.

Maneuvering for position in the service and for seating in

the large Cathedral was almost comical. When the majority and minority leaders of the House and Senate vied for positions closest to the coffin, it was an ironic reminder of how frequently, during his term as president, they had opposed his legislative initiatives and distanced themselves from him.

Yet the overall tone was somber. It seemed as if someone who had become a global navigator had disappeared, leaving those who'd come to rely on his bearings, adrift and uncertain.

In death, he began to be elevated to an almost iconic status. Global attention focused even more on the Template and implementing its principles.

And near universal interest seized the media in learning about the circumstances of his unexpected death.

CHAPTER 14

LOOSE ENDS

In the midst of public demands for information stood Special Agent Derrick Bone. The trouble was, although he had a tantalizing array of incriminating facts, none amounted to a smoking gun that proved anything. Just suspicions and innuendos. "Can't prove beyond a reasonable doubt on inferences and innuendos", he thought to himself.

That was about to change. As the day for the former President's Memorial Service approached, the airwaves and internet buzzed with speculation that Johnson's seemingly natural death was not. Talk show hosts on both sides of the political spectrum speculated openly, though with uncharacteristic gravity on the peculiarity of a fit man dying of a heart attack doing something he had done dozens of times before. Some analyzed what consequences his death would have on special interest groups. The Memorial Service was set for Sunday, a week following his death at Friendship Point. Early Wednesday morning, as Bone listened to a Bach Cantata while he did a two mile run shortened from his usual five, his pager went off. He checked and recognized the incoming number as that of Lydia Stonecraft.

Normally dedicated to finishing his run no matter what, he left the trail and pulled out his auxiliary cell phone to call her.

"Professor Stonecraft, this is Derrick Bone".

"Ah, yes, Mr. Bone", she began somewhat stiffly.

Her voice sounded strained as if she had been crying and

was trying to collect herself. It also sounded like she had been drinking.

"I….I don't know if it will make any difference to you, to your investigation", she paused.

"But I remembered something I didn't mention when we talked before about Joshua….I mean President Johnson's death."

Her reference to her close friend and mentor by his former title showed she was getting a handle, however tentatively, on a new reality that was taking over since Johnson died. This is good, Bone thought to himself.

"Anything could be helpful", he said encouragingly.

"Well, I remember that about three days before his death, the President had a dream- a premonition if you will - that something terrible might happen to him. He said that he dreamed that he had died and was looking down at his body lying in state. He told me Lincoln had such a dream just before he went to Ford's Theatre." She hesitated again.

"Of course he didn't assign any particular weight to it. Death threats had become commonplace to him – both as President and during his post president years when he was helping negotiate peace treaties in troubled areas. And the Template; well, you can hear from the 'Talking Heads' what a storm of dissent that aroused.

"Anyway", she continued, "I saw fit to pass this on to Monty Le Beau as head of the Secret Service detail so he could be on the lookout for anything out of the ordinary. I'm not superstitious, but I do believe that there are higher levels of consciousness than our rational thought processes can fully understand. I think Agent Le Beau started monitoring even more closely the activities of Joshua - I mean the President - including the preparation of his meals."

"Who did prepare the President's meals?" Bone inquired,

seeing if her answer was the same as he had gotten from Le Beau several days before.

"Oh, Jack Richers, his long time cook and friend," Stonecraft responded.

"He'd served the President during the White House years and followed him into his retirement. He knew the President's whims and eccentricities like only old friends can."

"What kind of eccentricities?" Bone persisted.

"Well, like craving a sardine and kosher dill pickle sandwich on pumpernickel before going to bed." Recalling this domestic detail caused Professor Stonecraft to chuckle, then just as quickly, her voice cracked. But she recovered.

"Anyway, I thought you ought to know about the dream."

"Anything else?"

"No. That's all. I just thought I should pass it along."

After hanging up, Bone finished his run. He reflected on the discrepancy between Monty Le Beau's description of Johnson's bland diet with Dr. Stonecraft's reference to sardines and pickle sandwiches. As he was doing warm down stretches, his cell phone rang. He knew it must be the Chief since he was the only person who had Derrick's auxiliary number.

"Bone, I just had an interesting message come in this morning. Couldn't get through to your other cell phone, so I tried your backup. Anyway, you remember an Arab Professor you talked to in New York? Well, we got a message this morning, he called and wanted to talk to you. Didn't have a way to reach you, so he called here."

Derrick got the number and immediately called Dr. Nakob in New York. Nakob picked up right away. He seemed to be waiting for the call.

"Dr. Nakob, Special Agent Bone of the F.B.I. here, I understand you called."

"Ah, yes, Special Agent. Thank you so much for calling me back. I received a most troubling phone call this morning from an acquaintance of mine at the National Institute of Science in Cairo."

"Yes", Bone sensed a breakthrough.

"It seems that the topic we were discussing the other day – you know about an internal electronic device - was correct. Such a device has been developed by a rogue scientist - an Egyptian, I am afraid."

"Yes", Bone waited anxiously.

"Well this acquaintance learned of a purchase and shipment of such a device by Al Qaeda to the United States."

There was a long pause.

"Yeah", Bone answered, sensing his heart rate increase, even though he had stopped running. Al Qaeda had been run to ground years before after masterminding the deadly attack on the World Trade Center in 2001. He hadn't heard their name in several years.

Nakob continued, "Anyway, my friend indicated that he believed the deadly device had been shipped to some celebrity in the U.S."

Celebrity in the U.S.? Bone thought, what kind of celebrity would have anything to do with Al Qaeda? It was a name that was still poison in the U.S. But it wouldn't be the first time that someone had dealt with the enemy, Bone thought, recalling the old saying "the enemy of my enemy is my friend." He remembered Oliver North in the Reagan Administration dealing with Ayatollah Khomeini's crowd in Iran to get illegal arms to the contras in Nicaragua in the 1980's.

"What celebrity?" Bone queried.

"Ah, that my friend was not sure of. But the object would have had to be specially shipped. It would require very careful handling."

"Why?"

"Well remember the way it works. It is triggered by an electric signal from a remote location. Because of its sensitivity, it could be triggered in shipment by any nearby electronic instrument on the right frequency thus destroying the device. And like some insects, once it stings it dies."

Bone considered what he'd need. "What's your source?"

"Please, Agent Bone, understand that if I share that with you and my friend is implicated, it could mean his death."

Recognizing the truth of this, Bone nevertheless persisted though on a different track. "When was the package shipped?"

"I understand about ten days before the President's death."

"From where?"

"Riyadh, Saudi Arabia."

"And he didn't have any idea who the celebrity was?"

"My friend didn't know. But he thinks it may have been someone in the media."

"Why is that?"

"Because he had heard something about broadcasting."

"Anything else?"

"No, I don't think so."

"Doc, thanks, you've been a great help. Stay in touch."

He gave Dr. Nakob his pager number and rang off.

Through secure channels, Bone immediately requested F.B.I. headquarters to check shipping records from Riyadh, Saudi Arabia within the last ten days to several major cities where major networks were based.

Then he called his friend Monty Le Beau.

The two old friends met in a park in Grand Rapids. Le Beau was winding down the security detail for the former President at Friendship Point. From the ashen look on his face, Bone could tell that Le Beau had spent several sleepless nights - though whether this was from grief or from anguish that a President had died on his watch was impossible to tell. Probably both.

Bone approached the subject as carefully as his blunt manner allowed.

"Monty, I had a call from Lydia Stonecraft this morning, she told me the President had a bad dream – a premonition about his death a few days before it happened."

"Yeah, that's right", Le Beau responded. He seemed distracted and distant.

"Anything you can tell me about that?"

"What's to tell? He had a bad dream. There were enough death threats to cause somebody in his position to have nightmares." He paused. "But just as a precaution, I began monitoring all aspects of his activity, even more closely. Even his food preparation."

"Why? You told me his cook had been with him forever."

"I don't know. I guess I'm just too much like you. When I'm onto something and think there might be danger to the guy I'm protecting, I get obsessive."

"Why didn't you mention this before?" Bone demanded.

"Didn't think it was necessary. Nothing out of the ordinary turned up."

"And you monitored his meal preparation right up to the night he died?"

"Well. Yes."

Then he hesitated.

"Well, except the night itself, he had a bowl of clam chowder about half an hour before he went in for his swim. Now that I think about it, I got called away on another security concern, so I asked Rodman to stand in for me."

"How well do you know Rodman?" Bone asked.

"We worked this security detail for the last year and a

half. He is over the top on some things. But never knew him to 'get political' if you know what I mean. Why?"

"Just asking. Trying to leave no stone unturned." Bone replied noncommittally. He didn't bring up the late night sandwich at this point – it appeared too remote in time to be the means for planting the device in any event.

He went back to the agency office and called the U.S. Attorney.

CHAPTER 15
INURNMANT

Funeral arrangements were changed at the request of family members and President Johnson's closest associate, Lydia Stonecraft. In keeping with his desires to conserve, the former President had decided his remains would be cremated instead of being buried. However, due to the outpouring of desire for people to pay respects, the body would be embalmed and placed in a simple pine coffin for the state funeral which Professor Stonecraft, with family backing, directed be a celebration of the late President's life and affirmation of his values. Stonecraft's visible role in the preparation gave grist to gossip columnists about the attractive professional's relationship to the late President. Since his wife had died five years earlier and they had no children, Stonecraft had assumed the role of Johnson's closest companion as well as collaborator. What's more, the former President's four siblings were scattered and, although not estranged from their celebrated brother, had seen little of him for the last several years due to his intense public schedule. They deferred to Lydia in making arrangements; though one of them was to speak at the service.

Meanwhile the search of shipping records from Riyadh was narrowed by a grid Bone devised concerning types of shipments and locations. Cities of choice narrowed to New York and Nashville – the former because of the concentration of media and Nashville because of its association with a couple of fairly extremist radio talk shows. Besides, Bone reasoned, the relative unlikelihood of business links between Riyadh, Saudi Arabia and Nashville, Tennessee seem to make shipments between these points of heightened interest.

Scanning records during the days in question and narrowing the search by association with entertainment or other media addresses, a startling location came up: Truth Seekers, LLC. This was Charlie Gasser's broadcast system, a far ranging enterprise of right wing business operations involved in everything from selling campaign services and marketing literature to bobble heads featuring Gasser's name or likeness.

The flagship of the operation was Charlie Gasser's daily radio program broadcast nationwide from his studio in Nashville. The connection seemed to defy belief, Bone thought. This guy is regularly attacking anything he perceives to be hostile to America – from liberal politics to what he refers to as "ragheads wearing explosive belts". It seemed almost inconceivable Gasser could actually be doing business with some of the very folks he daily excoriated.

"Almost" was the key word. For there it was; a shipping invoice with a Riyadh origin, small package – directed to Truth Seekers for "CG's eyes only". The invoice did not specify contents other than to indicate that it was fragile and contained electronic equipment. Equally extraordinary were the precautions taken in shipment, including delivery in an electronically shielded package, with mark up to prevent it from being scanned or x-rayed. Wouldn't this have triggered Homeland Security's alarm button? Presumably. But, Bone reflected, he'd heard of mock-up missiles being shipped from China in the early 2000's by an enterprising U.S. news organization intent on testing our border protections and the missiles sailed through.

If this was the mystery package and assuming Gasser

got it, what was the link to Churlish and Agent Rodman at Friendship Point? He knew Churlish was a regular guest on Gasser's program. Assuming he was in Nashville, the hand off could have occurred then. But would Churlish or Gasser, for all their angry talk, really be so radical or reckless as to get involved with plotting an assassination? It seemed almost inconceivable.

"Almost" again was the key word. These guys were on record claiming President Johnson was dangerous to "the American way of life". And with a technology so new as to be under the radar, it might be pulled off without suspicion or detection.

He knew he had to stop arguing with himself and stick to the facts. He checked to see if Churlish had been to Nashville for any of his appearances in recent weeks on Gasser's show before the President's death. He had, on three occasions; the last only three days before President Johnson's death. The visit coincided perfectly with the message on Rodman's answering machine announcing "the package has arrived".

Search warrants would be needed to check communications between Gasser and his contacts in the Middle East. This would draw a likely series of blasts from Gasser about "big brother butting his nose into honest folk's business". Or maybe not, if it would draw added attention to his own suspicious acts.

Ironically, as Bone mulled the evidence, he heard another agent's radio tuned to a time delayed broadcast of Gasser's latest show. In it he condemned "Mideast terrorist types; the sandal and bathrobe wearing raghead mullahs of madness who take our money and peddle hate for all things we hold dear". He continued, "they are still stuck in the Middle Ages trying to get even for our winning the crusades".

Beyond Gassers usual muddling of facts, Bone thought

it seemed like an odd choice of topics for someone who has taken a Muslim country's state of the art technology to perform his own act of skullduggery. Then, he reflected, it would be really nice to take down this S.O.B.

The U.S. Attorney - perhaps unsurprisingly, Bone thought afterwards – refused to obtain search warrants on the basis of the evidence accumulated to date.

"What's the proof this new device exists? And how do you know if it did exist, that it ever got within 100 miles of the ex-President?" he demanded. "How do you expect a federal court judge to believe that this 'almost undetectable' device was even in the President's system when he died? How can you prove it? And Al Qaeda and Charlie Gasser? Come on, that's pretty wild – just too wild".

Bone acknowledged there were missing links, however confident he was of his emerging theory. And with the planned cremation of the President's body, primary evidence could quite literally go up in smoke.

He needed to act fast. If there was any way to prove the presence of the deadly device in Johnson's system, he needed to secure it without delay.

After leaving the U.S. Courthouse, he called Dr. Nakob in New York to pick his brain.

"Doctor, you told me that a higher level of electronic activity in a victim's body was an evidence of the presence of the internal electronic device. How definitive could that be? Could it be treated as conclusive evidence one of these things had been planted and used?"

"Conclusively?" the Doctor cautiously asked. "I doubt it. There are other variables that could be at work to cause electronic outbursts."

Bone's hopes sagged.

"But" the Doctor continued, "there may be unique markers

indicating a quantitative and localized surge of electrical activity that could surpass anything naturally occurring within the human body by any other explanation. By elimination of other causes, one may establish the device's presence. I believe lawyers call this circumstantial evidence."

"Enough of which, can convict," Bone added drily. He jumped at the opening. "What kind of test could do this?"

"I'm not certain."

The rollercoaster ride continued.

"Probably a very sensitive electronic sensor - possibly modified from a C.T. Scan or an MRI – might demonstrate this. In science, measurements or outcomes are often determined by excluding other possibilities as much as proving one cause. The presence of black holes in space, for example, is demonstrated by the absence of any matter or of any alternate explanation."

MRI! Bone thought. An MRI had been performed on the body of the President. It didn't reveal much, he recalled. But maybe that was because they weren't looking for the right thing.

"Who would be able to make such a measurement? Can you suggest someone who would have the credentials to perform this testing and evaluate the results credibly?"

"Well, it's all very new; even experimental technology, so there are no established standards". He understood the thrust and importance of the F.B.I. Agent's questions.

"However, I believe that we could apply established principles in a corollary manner to detect the presence for use of one of these devices. And I think I know who can do it."

Agent Bone would have embraced the good doctor if they had been in the same room instead of half a continent apart.

Dr. Nakob identified himself and two associates at the University he felt could be both trustworthy and competent.

Bone reiterated the extreme sensitivity of the discussion and that the highest confidence needed to be maintained. Then he called the mortuary to put a hold on any embalming until after whatever testing needed to be done.

Within a half hour, Bone got a call from an outraged Lydia Stonecraft. Without bothering to introduce herself, she went on the attack.

"What do you mean putting a hold on Joshua's body? Who do you think you are? The whole world is waiting to pay tribute to the great and good work of this man; and you want to hold it up for more testing? What more could be done to the poor man's body? He's already been poked, prodded, and dissected." Her voice was white with anger as much personal as professional.

Bone had to be careful how he responded: say too much and he could compromise his investigation; too little and the furious woman might say something publicly that could jeopardize his efforts. With uncharacteristic tact, he appealed to the scientist.

"Professor, you are a person that cares deeply about making sure that you have things right, through testing and experimentation. Without being able to say more, let me just assure you that we wouldn't be holding things up if there weren't some extremely important tests to be run that could help answer the questions we talked about before; questions that you wanted answered and that the world deserves to have answered."

It was more than what he would normally say. But this was an investigation with greater ramifications than any he'd ever been involved with before. Such cases called for special measures. The last thing he needed now was the late President's closest confidant publicly criticizing his efforts.

The words hit their mark. She took his meaning.

"You've got a lead?"

"I can't say more than this; we need to do a couple more tests and it could be critical to nailing it."

Nail what – or who? Lydia wanted to ask. But she knew better.

"When?" She asked plaintively. "When will we know?"

"Soon."

She accepted his explanation and signed off; with the request – more a plea – that he find out what had happened to President Johnson and quickly.

* * *

The prior MRI scan was reviewed and key components identified where the electronic impulse readings were noted. A repeat MRI with intensified screening of the abdominal cavity was performed. This showed what Dr. Nakob and his associates confirmed to be a clear evidence of a major electronic outburst from a spot near the wall of the stomach that could not naturally occur from any other known cause. Almost imperceptible but visible traces of a low level burn of tissue had no alternate explanation. Bone had the team write up their report and fax it to him on a secure line at the F.B.I. office.

Bone's phone rang, it was the Chief. The call came in on his regular cell phone, not the backup line.

"Derrick, what the hell is going on?" The Chief demanded impatiently.

Bone's mind raced, the Chief knew he was not to be reached on this number because it was being monitored. He couldn't brief him on where things were – especially on this phone. But the Chief was sharp enough not to call the wrong number accidentally. If he was calling this number intentionally, then why?

The obvious reason made Derrick bristle. The investigation was getting close to some powerful people; people the Chief apparently didn't want to cross. But by using the compromised phone, he had chosen to give his agent a head's up.

"Bone? You there? What in hell's name are you doing? The U.S. Attorney called to ask me about a couple of warrants you wanted."

At least Chief Simpson didn't say who the warrants targeted, Bone reflected gratefully.

"Chief, I can't talk now, I'll call you back when I have something to report."

As he disconnected the call, he heard Simpson bark, "Bone don't hang up on me"...

But after Bone hung up, the Chief didn't call back. If he got a reprimand or worse, it was okay. The stakes were too high to stop or slow down now. Plus it was often easier to ask for forgiveness than for permission.

As he drove home, he realized he was being followed. He took several evasive measures, but the tail car stuck with him. Finally, he pulled into the parking lot of a nearby restaurant, went in and took a seat near the front window where he could see the parking lot without being seen. The tail car stopped across the street. There was only one person in it, although it was too dark to see more than a silhouette.

Derrick pulled out his backup cell phone and called an Assistant U.S. Attorney with whom he'd worked before and who had a reputation for being a real "tight ass" – a stickler for detail who was utterly incorruptible. Assistant U.S. Attorney Bill McCloud was said to follow a lead wherever it went, even if it meant indicting his own grandmother. To assure absolute impartiality, McCloud adhered what he had referred to as the "Marshall Doctrine": a military rule supposedly followed by General George C. Marshall, that he wouldn't even vote in an election to avoid expressing partiality towards any candidate or political party. Whatever Bill McCloud's higher ups may be doing in sharing information that could be compromising, Bone felt that McCloud would have no part of it.

McCloud, like Bone, had little life outside of the office. No wife, no kids, just work. Another thing I like about him, Bone thought. McCloud was also still up even though it was 11:00 p.m. and he would be at the office by 6:00 a.m. the next morning.

"Bill, this is Derrick Bone."

"What's up?"

"I need a couple of warrants."

Bone proceeded to briefly review the evidence gathered, from the missing presidential pager, freshly reviewed MRI scan showing evidence of foreign matter and electrical impulses, and records of a shipped internal electronic device from Saudi Arabia to Gasser's communication center in the U.S. Then he explained the properties of the internal electronic device and the timing of the mysterious communications between Rod Churlish and Secret Service Agent Rodman regarding a "package" arriving within days of the President's death.

There was a long silence at the other end of the line.

"What's the linkup between the Saudi shipment and the package arriving at Friendship Point?" McCloud asked.

This bothered Bone as well. He hadn't made the connection with hard evidence. But the elements were coming together. He needed to connect the dots.

"I don't have it yet", Bone answered ruefully.

McCloud finally asked with a touch of irony in his voice, "So, you want me to get a search warrant directed against a

Secret Service Agent assigned to a Presidential detail <u>and</u> a former National Security Advisor?"

Derrick paused, realizing the gravity of his request.

"Yeah, and one of the biggest voices in right wing radio. I guess that's about the size of it."

"You talked to my boss about this?"

"Yep."

"And what did he say?"

"He refused. Of course that was before we had the added MRI reading and opinions from several scientists familiar with how this nasty little assassination device is supposed to work. That and the electronic surge activity in the President's body which couldn't have come from any other known cause."

"Oh, and, your boss called mine. And mine called me on an unsecured line."

Another pause.

"So they're trying to tip someone off?"

"Seems like it. Now I'm sitting in a restaurant with a tail on my case and a bug on my phone and computer. Can you get me the warrants?"

McCloud, after another long pause, said he thought so. At least search warrants to build the case. <u>After</u> Bone got him his report.

Outside, a car turned the corner next to the restaurant. The headlights swept the vehicle across the street, lighting momentarily its interior. Bone recognized the driver. It was Dick Rodman.

Bone sighed in relief; the bench these bad guys have must be pretty shallow if a key suspect was doing his own cleanup work.

Agent Bone left the restaurant and drove to the F.B.I. office to file his report.

Johnson's memorial service would have to proceed

without his body. The wheels of justice grind out some strange results, he reflected.

He had the preliminary report completed and ready to deliver to the Assistant U.S. Attorney by midnight. He would hand deliver it in the morning. Meanwhile, he kept trying to get a linkage between the Saudi shipment to Gasser Communications and Michigan.

Swallowing a shot from the bottle of Wild Turkey he kept in his desk, he laid down on the couch in Chief Simpson's office for a one hour nap.

CHAPTER 16
PAYING RESPECTS

The funeral of a President or ex-President of the United States is unlike just about any other, except that of a long serving, well loved monarch or a popular figure who died young or unexpectedly. As head of state of a great world power, the funeral of an ex-President draws presidents, prime ministers, and potentates from around the world. Beyond the obvious purpose of paying respects, such events also afford the chance for political alliances to be subtly reinforced and thorny issues to be smoothed over, all in the context of mortality implicit in any funeral. Although still at some level a personal affair, these considerations inevitably predominated making Johnson's funeral very much an affair of state.

Thus, with or without the body of President Johnson, the service went forward.

In keeping with his wishes, that his body be cremated, it was understood there would be no viewing in state or otherwise. The pastor of the Lutheran church Johnson attended while at his retreat in Holland was asked to join the bishop of the National Cathedral, Johnson's church while president, in offering prayers and a message at the Memorial. But, narrowing the list of speakers somewhat from what was first planned, a rabbi, a Moslem imam and a Buddhist monk with whom the former President had worked were also asked to participate by Professor Stonecraft. This left President O'Brien and the U.N. Secretary General somewhat crowded between those offering memorials of a less worldly character than theirs would be.

Due to the ongoing investigation, the coffin ironically did not contain the remains of the man being honored. Instead, it had been weighted by simple stones equivalent in weight to the body of the missing president.

Of course no one suspected that while the somber service was conducted in National Cathedral, the former president's body was half a continent away in a laboratory in Grand Rapids, Michigan. Professor Stonecraft, one of the handful aware of the irony, felt President Johnson's presence in spirit, while silently grieving for her departed friend.

Prior to the funeral, she had come across a manuscript Johnson was working on when he died. It called for creation of a new organization, one he called the "Institute for Environmental Synergy". One part think tank; one part research facility, the Institute brought together two key elements in President Johnson's approach to life: education and problem solving.

In his proposal for the new organization, he wrote:

"The issue of climate change has come to be understood as the paramount challenge facing human life on the planet today. From rising ocean levels, to multi-year droughts; people experience displacement and hardship on a level unparalleled since the great Plague of the Middle Ages swept much of the world.

"Yet", he continued, "we have not fully fathomed the magnitude and consequences of the problems we face or the opportunities they afford for redesigning our life on this planet Earth."

"Realizing this, I propose we create an Institute of Environmental Synergy. It will have two primary missions:

"First, to operate as a not for profit educational

organization, working to better understand and explain the evolving array of challenges posed by climate change and environmental depletion. By study workshops, town meetings, traditional classroom training, and informational websites, the Institute will seek to raise the level of awareness about what we face and how to deal with these challenges locally and globally; and

"Second, it will run a for-profit research and development facility to explore new technologies and processes that address problems posed by climate change. The goal would be to do this with an eye towards thinking synergistically; in such a way that processes complement rather than compete with each other. For example, instead of merely producing an energy resource to power our cars and other motor vehicles on a stand alone basis, we could develop a central power source for our homes that could do this and heat or cool our homes as well. Solar thermal and photovoltaic systems could be conjoined to heat and cool our houses and work places; but also to charge hydrogen cells used to power vehicles during working hours. Waste streams from livestock operations on farms could likewise be recycled to produce both fertilizer to grow crops and methane gas to propel tractors and combines.

"Newly invented products and processes would be sold commercially to raise funds to finance further research as well as to promote the non-profit educational work of the Institute.

"In the end, we will imitate nature in sustaining life on our planet by processes that are both sustainable and complimentary.

"An initial problem with the Institute is to find a willing sponsor. With the accelerating pace of climate disasters, a market for the idea now exists.

"The second problem historically came from a conflict between protecting the right of the person coming up with a new useful invention and assuring the swift and widespread deployment of the invention into commerce. The Institute, in holding these proprietary rights, will be able to expedite this integration as a part of its core mission."

"The challenges are great. But so are the opportunities – economic, environmental, and political – that may come from the Institute."

Lydia read the brief manuscript carefully twice. Then she emailed it to each of the major networks and news organizations that Johnson had worked closely with in the months before his death. Editorial comments followed publication of the paper. Efforts to create Institutes in many countries followed. It was as if the President was reaching back from the grave to give one final message to the living. Paying respect to his memory seemed to many, little more than reciprocating the respect he showed those he left behind.

CHAPTER 17
SETBACKS

As Derrick waited for his search warrants to be issued, he received the shocking news of Professor Nakob's murder. Though initial details were sketchy, one of Nakob's assistants helping with the screening of the MRI data, called Bone to tell him of the death. He indicated that a note had been found in which Al Qaeda claimed credit for "punishing a traitor to holy Jihad". The assistant was frightened, afraid he may be next and begged for Derrick's help.

Al Qaeda, until recently a bad memory, was now not only active in exporting deadly new devices to the U.S., but was apparently able to act on American soil in eliminating a perceived enemy. Though Nakob had been targeted as a fellow Muslim, no one, including Bone himself, would be off limits. He notified fellow agents in New York to get witness protection for the lab assistants of Nakob, both of whom were themselves Muslims. As material witnesses to a criminal investigation, they clearly qualified for protection. If Al Qaeda knew of the existence of the MRI scan by Nakob and his two assistants, it was not beyond the realm of possibility that one of them could be the informant of the Al Qaeda cell in this country. In short, not only would these two witnesses need to be put in protection, but they would need to be kept separate and watched to make sure one of them wasn't providing further information that could compromise the investigation or other peoples' lives.

Alternately, could someone inside the intelligence agency

in Egypt have given the murderers information? Either way, if they were aware of Nakob's contact with Bone, they would be aware of the ongoing investigation of President Johnson's death and may be seeking to silence anyone who was collaborating.

And what was it that made Nakob a traitor in his murderer's eyes? That he'd disclosed the existence of the electronic device to Bone or that he'd assisted in the criminal investigation by examining the MRI? Bone had to assume both.

Suddenly, a whole different set of suspects surfaced from this scenario. Rodman's suspected one man cover up suddenly had a whole lot more participants.

The shipping invoices were incriminating and seemed to point in one direction. But what if Al Qaeda or some other foreign operatives were at work in this country on their own? What if they had secured copies of the records of the shipment aimed at the former President and were now attempting to claim credit for the deed themselves? They were clearly able to act in the United States – they had already eliminated one person they considered a foe.

What had seemed hours earlier a fairly straightforward investigation moving to an early conclusion now had all kinds of additional wrinkles that needed to be resolved and resolved quickly before there were any more deaths. The only good thing about the added developments was that it appeared that the conspirators were turning on themselves. This could make for some heightened opportunities for the good guys.

He wondered again how Rodman, Rod Churlish, or, for that matter, Charlie Gasser, could have had any conscious dealing with Al Qaeda. Aside from the natural aversion anyone with their backgrounds would seem to have in dealing with global terrorists; a range of security clearances surrounding at least Churlish and Rodman would seem to raise red flags for any suspected contacts. And true, Churlish and Gasser were slippery S.O.B.s; but it was hard to imagine that they could stoop that low. Was Bone barking up the wrong tree after all?

On the other hand, it occurred to Bone, that Gasser may be unaware of Al Qaeda's operation in the U.S. They would without doubt be monitoring Gasser's broadcasts and could only be outraged at his biting the hand that fed him – attacking "raghead mullahs". Should he warn Gasser?

No, Bone concluded: that would tip the hand of his investigation and could compromise its outcome. Besides, Gasser could face the consequences of his bombast on his own.

Bone got on the phone with McCloud to fill him in on what was going on.

Then he contacted the Department of Homeland Security where he'd worked before with Jennifer Jackson in the Special Ops Unit. If anybody was on top of what was going on with Al Qaeda in the U.S., she would be the one. She seemed surprised to hear from him and wary when she learned he was aware of Nakob's death.

"How did you know about Professor Nakob's murder?"

Bone replied, "He was a witness in an investigation we have underway."

"On what?" She queried.

At this point, the need to share information about an ongoing investigation – a bane of the intelligence community for years - kicked in. He felt an instinctive reluctance to share with her too many details of what he had underway just as she was obviously reluctant to share with him too much about what she was working on. Bone had been exasperated by this interagency communication breakdown for years. But the current situation made it all the more exasperating – and intolerable. Swearing under his breath, he filled her in on what he knew and where his investigation was going, right down to the last desperate phone call from Nakob's assistant telling him of what had happened, and seeking protective custody.

Thankfully, his directness prompted a similar response from Jackson. Her voice betrayed the shock she felt over what she had just been told.

Jennifer indicated to Derrick that they had isolated a newly activated cell of Muslim extremists, apparently associated with Al Qaeda, in the Detroit area. They were looking into connections between this cell and others in New York that could have been involved in Nakob's murder.

After sharing information, they agreed on a strategy for how to proceed together to flush out the killers.

CHAPTER 18
TRIANGULATION

Derrick met again with Assistant U.S. Attorney McCloud to review his additional evidence. Due to the intervening death of Dr. Nakob, Bone alerted McCloud of an Al Qaeda cell operating within the United States.

As for Charley Gasser, Bone's apprehension proved justified. The day after his broadcast blasting "ragheaded mullahs of madness", Gasser's armored limousine with his driver and two bodyguards were themselves blasted, as it left his gated mansion in Nashville. Amazingly, Gasser survived, though with second degree burns and deafness in both ears from the explosion. No one claimed immediate responsibility. But the bombing had all the earmarks of those that had regularly rocked the Middle East for many years.

McCloud went before the Federal Magistrate and got search warrants for Gasser's studio and home as well as Rod Churlish's home and office. Computer records at each reflected exchanges extending back over several months, cryptically referencing a "Green Dove" – presumably ex-President Johnson, and lacerating him for his environmental initiatives. Over the last month, these had grown more specific in focusing on the need to "stop him" before he destroys "everything we believe in".

Records also indicated a transfer of funds from Gasser's accounts to a Swiss Bank associated with money laundering for Arabic extremist groups. It appeared that Gasser, despite all his flourishes, was remarkably naïve in covering his tracks. Bone recalled other celebrities who had let their prominence delude them into thinking they were invulnerable and got careless with the trail they left behind - like Eliot Spitzer's electronic records of dealings with a prostitute, or Tiger Woods emails with women he cavorted with; all the way back to the granddaddy of them all, Richard Nixon's White House Tapes.

What surprised Bone was that Churlish hadn't been more careful.

But there was a missing link. How could it be proved that the electronic device went from Gasser to Churlish to Rodman? And did the surge of electric impulse in a person's body prove existence of an instrument of assassination – particularly when the device was as virtually unknown and untested as the electronic device? The assistants of Dr. Nakob could be helpful on this since they had knowledge of the scientific principles and test results on President Johnson's body. But they had no evidence that the instrument itself was in Johnson's body. Just like a roadside IED, the diabolical internal device apparently destroyed itself as it went off. There was no "smoking gun"; just circumstantial evidence – however compelling.

The breakthrough would come, he reasoned in getting Gasser or Churlish to crack to save their hides. Worked all the time in cases of conspiracy. But at this level? Why not? he thought. The stakes are high; the public's attention huge. And frankly the outcome would be pretty profound. Somebody was going to pay for this and, he knew guys like these will turn on each other in a heartbeat to cover their hides. Though Bone knew in his gut that he had the right people with the goods, his reason still doubted.

Assistant U.S. Attorney McCloud harbored fewer apprehensions. He seemed truly outraged that people in positions of public trust could be so arrogant as to plot to assassinate a former President of the United States. He felt confident that based on the information he had, he could at least get indictments from a grand jury. Yet, the nature of the crime and the dangers of the device were such that McCloud wanted to get arrest warrants without the delay of a grand jury.

Agent Bone appreciated McCloud's confidence in the case but wondered openly how to safeguard against future use of the deadly electronic devices. McCloud responded: "You said the national intelligence agencies have been working on this and that the devices are extremely sensitive to electronic interference. Why don't you just jam the damn things?"

McCloud had a point. Bone had heard from Nakob that the devices were very unstable and could potentially be set off by any electronic impulse. Hence the difficulty of transporting them and the need to strip the ex-President of his pager before he started to swim.

The noose was tightening. Given what the wiretaps revealed, Bone and McCloud decided to bring Gasser in for questioning first.

His injuries from the car explosion were not life threatening and gained the talk show host initial sympathy from his followers, and even the mainstream media. Playing off this when the search warrants were executed, he first threatened the U.S. Attorney with a very public condemnation in his radio broadcast: "harassing one of patriotism's strongest defenders for exercising his freedom of speech". But when it became apparent that this would only increase exposure of his misdeeds, he backed off.

Next he evoked his Miranda rights – the same ones he'd condemned for years on his radio broadcasts. So the lawyers got involved. That's okay McCloud reasoned: "When they know what we've got, Gasser's attorneys will be only too eager to cut a deal since his client will be looking at life without possibility of parole if he doesn't work with us. Conspiracy is a lot less serious offense than accessory to murder. And the link between Al Qaeda and Gasser? Imagine what his fans will think of that!"

As expected, Gasser proved to be far less brave when confronted with evidence of his contacts with Mideast terrorists than he pretended to be when confronting such organizations on the air waves. He was only too willing to lay the blame at the feet of Rod Churlish, who he almost pitifully characterized as his "political mentor and role model". Describing himself as a pawn of someone else, after he had worked so hard to manipulate others, struck McCloud as almost pathetic, though he was quite willing to exploit this weakness in furthering his criminal case.

Churlish was the next target of the energized Assistant U.S. Attorney.

Then the emerging case took another bizarre and unexpected turn.

Late that night after Gasser was brought in for questioning, Dick Rodman showed up on Derrick Bone's doorstep.

Looking disheveled and weary, Rodman seemed anything but menacing to the surprised F.B.I. Agent.

"Can I come in?" The weary looking Rodman asked softly.

Taken aback, Bone didn't at first know what to say. Given the ongoing criminal investigation, he realized any conversation without extending Miranda warnings could imperil use of whatever Rodman would tell him. Besides, this was more McCloud's territory as a prosecutor than it was Bone's as an investigator.

As if reading Bone's mind, Rodman volunteered. "It's okay. I know what's going on and I'll waive my Miranda rights if you want me to sign something. But there are just some things you need to know."

"I'll need to tape what you tell me", the still surprised Agent said almost reflexively.

The guy looked so obviously distressed that Bone waived the beefy Secret Service agent into his living room.

"That's okay", Rodman responded.

"I've been following your investigation into the late President's death." Rodman volunteered quietly.

The respectful choice of words in describing Johnson struck Bone as odd for someone involved in his assassination. Bone said nothing.

"I had your house wiretapped, and even went to the extent of trailing you a couple of nights ago. And I know about the search warrants issued for Churlish and Gasser. I expect you found out about the electronic device." Rodman paused.

"Nasty little device. Diabolically so," Rodman mused to no one in particular.

"I suspect you put together the chain of custody on the nasty little bugger, from the Saudi's to Gasser in Nashville to Churlish." He paused again.

"And then ultimately to me."

Bone felt the hair on his neck rising. Was this tough Secret Service agent about to make a confession? Or something else? The missing link appeared tantalizingly close to being delivered to Bone's doorstep.

After what seemed like five minutes of nerve wracking silence, the Secret Service Agent continued.

"The thing is, I couldn't go through with it. I didn't like the former President's politics and I tended to agree with Gasser and Churlish about the disastrous effect his policies could have on our country. But he was still a former President, and the person I was sworn to protect. It wasn't right what they planned to do."

Another pause.

"So when Churlish got me that lousy little piece of assassination machinery and the appointed time came to use it, I didn't do it."

What Rodman had just told him nailed the missing link in how the electronic device got to Friendship Point and the elements of the conspiracy. But if what Rodman said was true and he didn't use the device. Then who did?

Bone didn't go there yet.

"You are obviously up to speed on our investigation." Bone said sardonically.

"But, I'm left with two big questions," Bone paused.

"Yeah, and I bet I know what they are."

"Well, then why don't you answer them for me."

"First, you wonder if what I say is true why I would have wiretapped or followed you."

"Yeah, that's one."

"I needed to know where your investigation was going. When I sabotaged the plot, I figured that was it. Then when the President died just like we had planned, even though I hadn't planted the electronic device, I needed to know what had happened. Who did this to the guy I was supposed to be protecting, or was it just a freak heart attack like everyone initially said?" Rodman pressed on with a tone of urgency to his voice.

"Yeah", Bone responded dryly. "Given your concern for Johnson's well being I bet that was a big worry."

Rodman ignored the remark.

"Second, you want to know how I can prove I didn't go through with the plan", Rodman replied.

With that, the Secret Service Agent put on a latex glove

and reached into his right suit coat pocket pulling out a tiny box, no bigger than a contact lens case though considerably better insulated. He set it on the coffee table.

"Have a look. That is the electronic device that Gasser bought from the Arabs and Churlish gave to me."

Bone reached out to pick it up; but the Secret Service agent grabbed his wrist and handed him a pair of latex gloves.

"Want to keep fingerprint evidence", he quietly reminded the F.B.I. Agent.

After pulling on the gloves, Bone examined the small box with a microscopically small detonation device in it.

Then he thought to himself, well, we needed the smoking gun. Now we've got it. Only trouble is, it isn't smoking.

CHAPTER 19
NEW ANGLES

Agent Rodman's confession confirmed the existence of a conspiracy to assassinate the former President. But it raised a whole new question about who had actually carried it out, assuming it was an assassination, which now appeared in serious question. Reviewing with Rodman the evidence of that fateful night at Friendship Point, Rodman confirmed he had covered for Monty Le Beau during the evening before the President set out for his fatal swim. But he had left the house briefly about the same time a food service delivery supplier from Grand Rapids arrived at the cottage. He remembered the service company's name was "All American Catering" – a name that struck him as strange given the strong accents and Mideastern appearance of the caterers themselves. He had only been gone about five minutes and the President's long time chef had been in the kitchen the entire time he was gone. Rodman also recalled how excited the caterer's seemed to be about delivering food supplies to a former president.

The chef had seemed a little nervous and out of sorts that night. But Rodman was sufficiently preoccupied with the conspiracy he was unilaterally aborting that he didn't pay too much attention to the chef's demeanor.

"These caterers seemed almost zealously pro-American – talking enthusiastically about their forthcoming citizenship exams." Rodman hadn't thought much of it. In his years of covering Presidents, he'd heard it all, from those eager to trash the U.S. and all it stood for, to those ready to offer their lives for the republic. Until recently, he'd clearly seen himself in the latter category.

Bone pushed him: "Tell me about the chef. I understand he was the President's long time cook and even a personal friend."

"Above reproach." Rodman confirmed, "If left to his own devices. But anyone can be turned."

He paused; did Bone detect a slight blush in the crusty Secret Service agent's face at the admission?

He continued, "If his loved ones were threatened he is very close to his aged mother and a couple of spinster sisters. It's a possible angle that could have been played."

But what would they have pressured him to do? Bone thought to himself. There is no evidence the ex-President was poisoned. And the electronic device was laying on the coffee table in front of him.

He remained inwardly outraged that Churlish, Gasser, and Rodman could have hatched their plot. But Rodman's forthrightness – and presentation of the hard evidence of the device– tempered his anger at least for the Secret Service agent.

"Anything is possible – but it is a hell of a coincidence that the President died that same night." Bone observed to no one in particular.

"Yes and no," Rodman continued. "Some Arabs wanted to get rid of President Johnson because he was building bridges between the U.S. and Muslim countries through his environmental initiatives – and by his willingness, which I didn't always agree with – of treating Muslims as equals. They hated him because he was stealing their thunder."

"Besides, if they could claim credit for killing an ex-president on his home turf, it could show that they could go wherever they wanted and do as they pleased. It could shake up a whole lot of people, here and abroad."

"Yeah, including me," added Bone.

"But what is the point of the electronic device that kills somebody but makes it look an accident or heart attack? If you want to publicly flex your muscles you don't set it up to look like an accident. You want it to look more like the attempt on Gasser's life." Bone caught himself. In his eagerness he'd let slip that Gasser's near miss was the work of Arab terrorists, a fact shared with him by Jennifer Jackman at Homeland Security.

Rodman seemed unfazed. "That was foreign terrorists? I figured it was just another of Charlie's numerous enemies."

"They must not have liked being called 'ragheaded Mullah's", Bone drily remarked seeking to change the subject.

"Anyway," Rodman continued with a trace of bitterness in his voice, "The beauty of that deadly little device", he said gesturing towards the small box on the table between them, "is that it allows you to claim credit or pretend it was an accident, as suits your need of the moment."

Bone had heard enough. He asked Rodman if it was understood that the electronic device was now in official custody, which Rodman confirmed. Then he stood up.

Rodman, apparently expecting to be placed under arrest stood up and extended his hands.

Bone looked at him.

"Yeah, I could put you under arrest. Probably should. But you attempted to thwart the plot. Besides you could do more good where you are than where you'd be if I put you under arrest. I'm betting you'll be contacted by Rod Churlish. So you are free to go. But I am going to want you to wear a wire."

After a brief exchange, Rodman left Bone's home equipped with a wire and a mission to visit with the former National Security Advisor.

CHAPTER 20
PARTINGS

The memorial service in Washington was carried over all major network, cable and print organizations, evidencing the global status of Johnson. Coverage and commentaries surrounding the service indicated that he had truly come to be seen as more than a representative of the United States. Like certain other figures in history – Lincoln, Martin Luther King, Jr., or Mahatma Gandhi - he seemed to symbolize something common to the aspirations of people around the World. And the tributes, if belated, were profuse. Lydia Stonecraft found herself at once exhilarated and depressed at the outpouring. So much could have been accomplished if people had embraced his ideas earlier while he was alive... her thoughts drifted off in a melancholy direction.

Awareness of Bone's investigation helped keep her focused during the difficult days of parting – with family, longtime associates, even heads of state who had grown to know her through the late President.

She found her thoughts continuously drawn, as if by a powerful magnet to the progress in the investigation. From a scientific perspective, this made little sense: nothing the investigators turned up would return Joshua to her. Likewise, determining there was foul play in his death would almost diminish it: As if a good and noble life had fallen prey to mankind's sordid nature, like the assassinations of Gandhi or Dr. King. Yet she felt compelled to know what had happened to her dear friend and mentor. She restrained herself for two days after her last visit with Bone, when he tantalized her with the suggestion of a forthcoming break in the investigation. Finally, she called again.

Bone, never a diplomat was taken aback by the call.

The conversation started innocuously enough with Lydia asking if there had been any new breakthroughs since they had last talked.

Bone, always wary of sharing any information, was coy.

"Well, yes there have been. But I'm not at liberty to say more right now."

Disappointment and frustration were apparent enough in Lydia's response that Bone amplified slightly.

"As I mentioned when we spoke last time, we're pursuing some promising leads. But I really can't say more until..." He cut himself off.

He'd confirmed evidence of a crime, and that was more than he intended or desired to divulge. Yet, given developments of the last 36 hours – Nakob's death, the bombing of Gasser's car, the bombshell of Rodman's confession – Derrick was sorting out all the new angles for his investigation.

The professor was persistent. "I understand that you need to keep things confidential while the investigation is underway. But I need to know something - anything - to clarify how this tragedy happened. I'm coming to Holland early next week to begin closing things up at Friendship Point. I'd like to meet with you."

Bone cautiously agreed, sensing her perspective might lend some insight that could be helpful to the still unfolding investigation.

CHAPTER 21
TOO MANY COOKS

With Rodman's confession – and proof of the unused electronic associated device – Bone's attention returned to Friendship Point and President Johnson's cook. As the longtime friend and trusted retainer of the late President, it was almost inconceivable Jack Richers could have knowingly had anything to do with Johnson's death. But then this case seemed filled with the inconceivable; from national security advisors involved in assassination plots, to talk show "patriots" consorting with Mideast terrorists. It was always possible, as Rodman had suggested, that the good chef had been threatened or coerced into cooperating with criminals. But the loyalty the late President had shown towards him and his reciprocal affection for the President, made this unlikely.

Bone returned to the scene of the crime once again, this time to interview the cook about the events of the evening of Johnson's death. Richers was distraught. It developed that he had been married years before to a woman who had shared his love of cooking and operated with him a restaurant in Grand Rapids known whimsically as the "Velour Feed Bag"; refined dining in a homespun setting. Joshua Johnson and his late wife, had been regular customers of the restaurant before his Presidency. Then the restaurant was destroyed in a freak gas explosion, killing Jack's wife. When Johnson learned of the tragedy, he invited the chef to come work for him in Washington. He had remained with Johnson throughout his presidency and beyond, up to the day of his death.

The cook had no idea that foul play was suspected in the death of his friend and patron. When Bone introduced himself as with the F.B.I., the cook's eyes widened in surprise.

Bone carefully reviewed the events of the evening Johnson died. Richers responded eagerly, almost effusively; as if by talking about it, he might somehow at least mitigate the outcome. Yes, the President was regular in his routine and eating habits on Sunday evening. He loved his clam chowder and preferred it with a little Cayenne pepper to spice it up. He just had a cup. A bigger meal with the rest of his staff would follow his swim. Although he liked good food, moderation was one of the President's hallmarks.

Richers also recalled the caterers arriving around dinner time. Yes, he remembered they appeared foreign, but that meant little; as the late President with his worldwide outlook welcomed folks of differing nationalities to his home and frequently spoke proudly of America being "a nation of immigrants."

The chef also recalled these caterers being very enthusiastic about delivering food to the home of the great ex-President. Several of them emphasized "the honor" this represented to them because they were great admirers of President Johnson and the United States.

Bone asked if he noticed anything unusual about the group.

Richers responded "Nothing really besides their enthusiasm and their number. There were five or six of them – usually only two or three would come to deliver food, unless they had a large banquet to prepare."

Then he paused.

"There was one fellow, now that you mention it; who seemed a little aloof from the others. He didn't say much and didn't seem to share the enthusiasm of the others."

"What did he look like?"

"Fairly young – mid-20s I'd guess. Very serious. Mideastern of course.

"What were you doing while they delivered the supplies?" Bone asked.

"Cooking the president's chowder and laying it out on his tray."

"Did you leave the room at all while the caterer's were there?

"No, of course not."

"What do you mean?"

"The Presidents or ex-Presidents get a lot of hate mail, the Secret Service have their job. I have mine. Both are to assure the good health and security of the man we care for."

An interesting attitude, Bone thought. Could be a case of protesting too much. But the cook's track record with Johnson suggested otherwise. He pushed another angle.

"Five or six people? How long were they here?"

"Ten, fifteen minutes tops – basically just to deliver food and stock it in the freezer."

"Did you supervise this?"

"Yes, of course. There were a few new faces who didn't know their way around."

"They'd delivered food before?"

"Oh yes. Did a good job; and it made the President feel good to be helping newcomers to our country"

"So you might have shown a couple of them where to put things while the others stayed behind?"

"Yes, I suppose that's right."

The cook's face fell as he said this. It had obviously just dawned on him that he would have been distracted from the food on the stove or even on the serving tray while he was in the freezer.

Bone sensing his reserve, shifted subjects. "I suppose the Secret Service kept a manifest of everyone coming and going from the compound."

The chef appeared flustered for the first time in their interview.

"I...I suppose so. I'm sure they must."

Bone thanked the cook for his help. As if to reassure him, he added he wanted to try some of that clam chowder the next time he visited.

Then he contacted Monty Le Beau to check the manifest of those entering or leaving the compound.

CHAPTER 22
JIHAD

Professor Stonecraft arrived a day early, and called Bone from the airport in Grand Rapids. He was not pleased. Bone had gotten hold of the manifest after the meeting with the Chef and had run the names of the caterers through the F.B.I. computer to look for matches with anyone on the Terrorism Watch List. There had been one match up; but with the most common of Muslim names – "Muhammad Ahmed". Kind of like finding a Don Johnson in Minneapolis. The positive match meant little. Further cross checking of photos and fingerprints for DNA - on the odd chance the signer on the registry had left fingerprints - would be needed.

In the meantime, he'd updated Assistant District Attorney McCloud of his findings and was having tracers put on the movements of any Muhammad Ahmed in the F.B.I. and Homeland Security Registry.

McCloud was running into resistance as he pushed his investigation of Rod Churlish. Better at bluffing and stone-walling from his years at global politics than his radio counterpart, Churlish scorned news of Gasser's betrayal in pointing the finger at Churlish. Telling the District Attorney's office to "piss off" when they called to set up a time to talk, Churlish and his now constant lawyer companions had obviously determined to force the D.A. to get hard evidence – not the panicky confessions of a radio talk show "blowhard", as Churlish now labeled his former confederate. What's more, due to his newfound reticence to speak out, Churlish cut off

Agent Rodman, assuring the wire he wore to record their conversations went nowhere.

In short, what Bone didn't need right now was to be distracted by a very upset and grieving friend of the former President giving him the third degree.

Still, he reasoned, she may be able to shed some added light on some phase of the investigation. "And I told her to call if she needed to talk" he reflected.

Bone had forgotten what a striking woman Lydia Stonecraft was. He'd seen pictures of her with the former President, but this was the first time he had met her in person. Tall, slender, and athletic, she had thick raven hair and a Mediterranean olive complexion. But her most compelling feature was her lively blue eyes, clearly animated by a quick and intense mind.

"In other circumstances..." Bone thought to himself sardonically; realizing his professional duties - as well as the social gulf separating them: he a local F.B.I. gumshoe, and this woman, the confidant of presidents.

Yet she had, after all, called him, and not the other way around.

Ah, the humbling affect of needing something only one person can give, he thought to himself wistfully.

For her part, the Professor began the conversation in a disarming fashion with an apology for arriving early.

"But", she explained. "Your reference to progress in your investigation and identifying a suspect piqued my interest. They drove me out of Washington as soon as Joshua's memorial service was over."

"What have you learned that you can share with me?" she prodded as tactfully as circumstances allowed.

Bone tried to return her gaze coolly. Yet he suddenly felt

an odd self consciousness that was both unsettling and out of character for the grizzled G-man.

He cleared his throat, feeling an almost adolescent impulse to share with her details of his investigation – as if to impress her with what he'd learned.

But, ingrained professional restraint checked the impulse. Instead, he chose a middle course.

"I never actually told you there was a criminal investigation. Just that we were following up on leads", Bone corrected her.

Her face fell. More bureaucratic stonewalling, she thought to herself. Give me some patience with this hard headedness.

Bone continued, "Actually, I wanted to talk to you about a couple of things."

He figured the best way to counter her curiosity would be to get her talking about what she knew – some of which may prove helpful to the investigation. It might also help overcome the uncomfortable distraction he felt talking to her one on one in person.

"What can you tell me about Jack Richers, the President's cook?"

Professor Stonecraft looked bewildered at the question.

"Jack? Why he was like a member of the President's family. Closer actually" - a comment she felt uniquely qualified to make having dealt with Johnson's siblings over the last few days of Memorial preparations.

She shared essentially the same story Bone had heard before from Monty Le Beau about the explosion and fire destroying the chef's restaurant and leaving him a widower.

Then the Professor prodded, "But surely you're not suggesting Jack had anything to do with Joshua's death? He would sooner die himself than do anything to jeopardize the President's safety."

Bone ignored her question.

"What about family members? I understand Richers may have had a close relative who was ill? Could someone have gotten to him through the relative?"

"You mean by threatening a loved one? Pressure Jack into doing something?" the Professor added. "No – definitely not. But why would you even ask that? Was there some evidence of food poisoning? I thought it was a heart attack? That's what the Medical Examiner's Report said."

The Professor's look of distress was giving way to anger that a close friend of the President was being impugned, and without any good or apparent reason.

Bone avoided the questions, "We are simply pursing all leads. We've got to do it."

"Well that lead seems to me like a perfect dead end", Stonecraft replied icily.

"Yeah, I think you're probably right", Bone conceded.

He didn't consider the chef as anything more than a well intentioned bystander who'd possibly been manipulated by others intent on getting at the late President.

"But tell me more about President Johnson. You told me earlier he'd had a dream about dying a few days before it happened. Did he tend to be superstitious or given to clairvoyant...suggestions?"

Stonecraft's face softened again, comforted to be talking about her old friend and mentor.

"Oh no, he really wasn't the least bit superstitious. He had strong religious beliefs about which he and I often debated. I suppose some of my colleagues may have seen his faith as superstitious. But I came to realize it was the thoughtful and deliberate conviction on which his whole life – public and private - was founded. He sometimes referred to his political work as 'witnessing' to his faith, in an almost Biblical sense of the term.

"As for clairvoyance", Stonecraft continued, "I assume you mean by that a belief in an ability to foretell events before they happen; Joshua would have laughed at the idea and argued 'history repeats itself often enough that if you give me a set of circumstances and a little background on the people involved, I'll tell you what is going to happen'.

"But as far as astrology or having a six sense, about as far as he'd go in that direction was to acknowledge the complexity of the human mind and its capacity for dimensions we might consider rationally impossible. He was really remarkably flexible in his openness to new ideas and directions, for someone so seasoned by political experience and the cynicism it usually brings."

"So would he act on these insights or premonitions?" Bone inquired.

"It would probably depend on the source and the context" the Professor answered deliberately. "As for the dream, no. As I told you before, I think he had grown so accustomed to threats and anger from those whose feathers he ruffled that he'd come to be quite philosophical about them."

"And what about those threats? You told me before that there were some groups particularly hostile towards him. Anyone in particular?"

She looked at Bone carefully. Then averted her eyes to stare at her hands folded on the table between them.

"It would be hard to say. Over the years there were so many. A lot of them just blowhards venting anger at a world leader because he was a leader."

"Blowhard". Bone thought to himself. He'd heard someone else use that term recently to describe Charlie Gasser.

"But there were a few who just kept coming back, day

after day and year after year. It's sort of a difference between the person who erupts in anger and it just blows over versus the person who does a slow burn, nursing resentment and lashing out in increasing viciousness over time."

"Like who?"

"Well, naturally some of the hate-headed radio talk show hosts like Charlie Gasser."

Her mention of Gasser's name hit Bone like a punch to the gut.

"But some of those in the foreign policy area just had a completely different world view than Joshua. They harbored a special malice towards him; as if their view was right, his was wrong, and there could be no middle ground. They felt his perspective had to be eliminated."

"Eliminated?" The word caught Bone's attention. "How do you mean?"

"Well, almost like the religious extremists of Islam waging Jihad, a few folks supposedly on our side had extreme ideological views. It almost seemed for them a holy cause or crusade – that their opposition needed to be entirely wiped out. It's insane, isn't it: extremists on our side face extremists on the other side and a whole lot of innocent people trying to find a middle ground in between, get killed."

"You thinking of anyone in particular?" Bone asked, "Anyone who threatened the late President with physical harm?"

Stonecraft drew herself up and looked Bone straight in the eye with a penetrating gaze.

"I wasn't part of those conversations. You'd have to talk to your friend Monty LeBeau for that information, Agent Bone."

Bone, wondering how the Professor knew of his past friendship with Le Beau, took this opportunity to end their conversation.

"And that is what I need to get back to."

CHAPTER 23
POLARITY

Knowing of the dead end with the Gasser-Churlish conspiracy as a result of his visit with agent Rodman, Bone went back to headquarters to see what the search of Muhammad Ahmed's records had turned up.

Homeland Security's records, released to Bone at Jennifer Jones' direction, traced the Muhammad Ahmed on the Terrorist Watch List to the Detroit, Michigan area. This individual had been born to a well to do Egyptian family and exposed to radical Islam tenets through his father's then-fashionable interest in the Muslim Brotherhood. While his father had come over time to view this organization as a vaguely idealistic and ultimately dangerous band, the son harbored no such disillusionment. He wandered first to the militant and ultra conservative Wahhabism of Saudi Arabia and ultimately to the Madrassas of northwest Pakistan. There he had combined belief in a beleaguered and persecuted Islam with military training in arms and explosives by elements of Al Qaeda. Though still young – he was in his early-twenties- he had already been exposed to a remarkable range of Islamic extremist influences. And, Bone reasoned, had developed a trail of connections he could tap when the circumstance required.

The Egyptian connection was particularly intriguing, given the Egyptian intelligence on the electronic devices Professor Nakob had provided. Could Ahmed have gotten his hands on one of those nasty little devices the same way

Gasser did? He wouldn't have had the money unless he was funded through Al Qaeda or some similar terrorist organizations. Due to his radicalism, Ahmed's father had long since cut him off from family support.

Chasing down the Detroit connection, the FBI had traced Ahmed to a number of extremist Imams and three mosques in the southeast Michigan Area. He had taken on a number of jobs, most recently in western Michigan with a Muslim owned and operated catering service. Its name – All American Catering – reflected the almost over-the-top patriotism of its Lebanese owners who had become naturalized citizens. Perhaps because of the business' strong support of patriotic and civic causes, Ahmed had apparently slipped though the screening that would customarily prevent access to a president or former president.

Ahmed had motive and access. But how could he establish Ahmed's control of the suspected instrument of death – the wretched, elusive, and minuscule electronic device? Professor Nakob, his lead into the Egyptian intelligence community was dead, apparently at Al Qaeda's hands. Ahmed, if he did get access to the device, could have done so theoretically anywhere, from Cairo to Riyadh to the Punjab in Pakistan.

Bone scowled. We'll need to bring him in and try to get him to confess. But these religious zealots were a strange lot. Often the more pressure applied, the harder they became to crack.

The first problem would be to find the guy.

Perhaps not surprisingly, Muhammad Ahmed had not reported for work in the days since President Johnson died. Traces and inquiries revealed he had disappeared seemingly into thin air. All American Catering provided an address, where the landlord informed the Agent that he hadn't seen his reclusive tenant "for at least a week". The Mullahs at the local mosques he frequented were reluctant to say anything to the F.B.I. Ultimately they provided little of value.

Terrorists seldom make many friends, Bone reasoned. They figure they are just passing through and don't want to call attention to themselves or distract from their missions.

But Ahmed had met a woman. Cybil Lockerbie was a blonde, blue eyed graduate student in the Islam Studies Program at Wayne State University. While first integrating into the Detroit Islamic community and before relocating to Grand Rapids, Ahmed had met Cybil at the library at Wayne State. Drawn to her by her name - so reminiscent of the terrorist - caused airline disaster over Scotland years before - he struck up a conversation with her over their shared interest in the Koran's teachings on holy war. Cybil was writing her doctoral dissertation on the Christian concept of "Just War" comparing it to the Islamic concept of "Jihad". Though coming from strikingly different backgrounds, Lockerbie and Ahmed had hit it off and developed what she described as a "trusting relationship".

When brought in for questioning by the F.B.I., she was stunned at first. Then defensive. Then she became combative on behalf of her friend. Bone was getting nowhere.

Finally Cybil referred to her sadness at the death of President Johnson - "one of the great men of our time". She alluded to the fact that she'd been "seriously bummed" since he passed away so unexpectedly a week before.

Bone saw an opening.

"Yeah, he was a pretty remarkable guy. Bone prompted in a conversational tone. "Sounds like he was doing some powerfully good work on the environment."

Eager to switch directions in the investigation and unsuspecting of her interrogator's motive, Cybil took the bait.

"Oh, I know. His Template made such good sense; and

the rash of recent environmental disasters just showed how overdue it was."

"The idea of an Institute of Environmental..." Bone began.

"Synergy" Cybil finished the sentence. "Yes it is an awesome idea – tying together market principles with scientific research and education. Makes so much sense."

Bone paused, allowing Cybil's obvious enthusiasm to sink in.

"Actually, our investigation of Muhammad has to do with these initiatives.

He paused again.

Cybil looked at him inquiringly. She was obviously surprised at the connection.

"I don't understand", she said.

"Well, since we are in the middle of an investigation, I can't tell you too much, but we need to talk to Muhammad because of some things that have happened that may..." he hesitated, "that may have jeopardized Johnson's initiatives".

Cybil still stared at him, more confused than ever.

"But Muhammad always told me he shared my concerns about the environment. He hated that our dependence on foreign oil had not only brought 'infidels' into Islamic holy lands, but was polluting the air we breathe for decades to come.

"I just can't imagine him doing anything to hinder environmental reforms."

"That's why we need to talk to him; to find out what he may know about serious efforts to impede Johnson's initiatives" He paused to let the words sink in, then he asked, "How long has it been since you last saw him?"

Cybil glanced nervously at the F.B.I. Agent. She paused. Then said "two days ago."

Two days! Bone thought excitedly. Maybe the trail hasn't

grown cold. He controlled his outward expression to suggest this came as no great surprise.

"Where was that?"

"He was passing through Detroit. Said he was catching a flight to Egypt to see his family."

That'll get him nowhere, Bone thought. Homeland Security and the F.B.I. both have him on a watch list to stop him at any airport.

"Did he say when he was leaving?" Bone asked nonchalantly.

"He said he was leaving in a couple days – said he had some unfinished business to wrap up here; looking in on some old friends I think."

"Did he say where he was staying?"

"Is Muhammad in trouble?" Cybil asked.

For the first time she seemed less concerned about defending her friend and more about finding out what he may have done.

"We don't know yet. That's the purpose of our investigation. Anything you can give us to locate him could clear things up and avoid causing added problems if he is in the clear."

Cybil glanced nervously again at Bone.

"He told me he was staying with a cousin downtown".

"Got a name or address?"

She gave him both.

Within the hour, Muhammad Ahmed was in F.B.I. custody.

CHAPTER 24

CONFESSIONS

Ahmed was not what Bone expected. Given his extreme ideology, his clean shaven face and western clothing seemed out of character. His demeanor was cool, almost relaxed, and seemed unconcerned that he'd been brought in for questioning by the F.B.I. Only his eyes, betrayed his intensity and anger. Over the years, Bone had come to believe the old adage that "the eyes are the windows of the soul". He'd rarely found a person whose eyes didn't reveal the character of the person within.

Bone wondered that this intensely angry man could have made friends with the gentle Cybil Lockerbie, whose description of Ahmed had conjured images of a reflective soul more interested in philosophy than fatwahs.

Yet, Bone reflected, his contacts with terrorist types in the past had yielded just such split personalities, the ability to project an almost domestic familiarity to a trusted few while seeing the rest of the world with intense hatred.

A tough interrogation would doubtless follow.

Ahmed surprised him.

After scornfully interrupting Bone's introduction, he made a blunt declaration:

"Do not patronize me. I know what you want and I'm proud to tell you what I've done. Begin your recorder and I will tell you as well who helped me do it. It will show you and the world the fatal corruption and decadence of your

Western way of life that will clear the path for rebirth of the Caliphate."

This reference to Islam's golden age was almost as frequent a reference in certain Islamic circles as the yearning for the Second Coming in certain Christian gatherings, Bone reflected. So he just listened, staring intently into the angry black eyes that met his.

"You crusader dogs have sought to infiltrate our holy places. Now we return the favor. You worship money, so we targeted your World Trade Center on 9/11. You worship power, so we have brought down your mightiest leaders."

"Getting close", Bone thought to himself, "This guy's about to spill it". The tape was running, as it had been since Ahmed began his tirade.

"We simply needed to choose the one."

For a moment, Ahmed glanced down at his hands as if his intense concentration had been broken.

"We foot soldiers of the holy war do not allow ourselves to be close to others; since we know a glorious death awaits us at any moment. We are prepared to be patient or to move swiftly." He paused.

"But when interference with the struggle in Somalia to establish a new Caliphate occurred, we knew what we must do."

Bone must have looked puzzled for the first time. He was. What did Somalia have to do with anything?

Reading the confusion on his listener's face, Ahmed proceeded contemptuously.

"See? You do not even know where Somalia is."

This wasn't quite true. Bone did have a general idea – some place in eastern Africa. He just no idea what it had to do with his investigation.

"We had started a mighty uprising in Somalia against

pirate warlords who sought mere plunder. After infidels and their collaborators defeated the Islamic States in Iraq and Syria, we planned to build a new center of Islamic power in the Horn of Africa – a place infidels consider a wasteland and desert just as they did Saudi Arabia until oil was discovered."

Bone remained certain this was leading somewhere, but the young zealot's rambling narrative had just taken him halfway around the globe from the investigation's focus. Bone recalled reading something about a pirate civil war going on in Somalia a couple of years before. But the story hadn't gotten much coverage. Just another intertribal quarrel between bad guys killing each other off on the far side of the globe.

But Ahmed was deep into his story.

"Then along came your President Johnson." Ahmed spat out the last two words with contempt.

"He destroyed our revolution by getting the corrupt Syrian government and Saudi princes to back the warlords we were fighting and bought off our supporters by bringing irrigation to this ancient desert region. Our leader, Hussein Ali, was ruthlessly killed in the struggle that followed. I resolved his murder would be avenged.

"You should understand this, as your religion teaches 'an eye for an eye'". The young man sneered at his interrogator.

"So we waited for the opportunity. And then, Allah be praised, a gift fell into our lap."

Bone must have leaned forward at these words, because Ahmed did likewise.

As their eyes met only six inches apart, Ahmed dropped his bombshell.

"We learned a new tool of holy retribution had been developed by our Arab scientists. Something small enough to be undetected by your scanners and testing devices, yet able to end the lives of our enemies."

Ahmed seemed to relish the words.

"And as we sought to obtain one of these for our purposes, we learned one of your celebrities had purchased two of them for an undisclosed sum."

Bone was hearing some things he already knew, if from a totally unexpected source. But the news of a second electronic device took him by surprise.

Ahmed searched the agent's face for signs of surprise and found none. Bone had developed an aptitude for expressionless through years of investigations taking unexpected turns.

"But the dogs who sold these devices to the Americans would not make them available to us. So we prepared other strategies of revenge. I obtained documents to get into the U.S. and came to Detroit to plan our next move."

The young man's eyes glittered malevolently as he continued his story.

"Our Mullah in Detroit knew of the Madrassa from which I came in Pakistan. He told me of a contact here; someone in politics who despised President Johnson almost as much as we did. So we arranged a meeting."

Bone at last interrupted, "and who was this American official?" He sounded skeptical.

Ahmed looked at Bone with disdain at his interruption. He ignored the question.

"We met. We spoke of our common hatred of the evil Johnson. He told me his values and my own were not so different; we both realized there is good and evil in the world and you must take a side. Those who try to compromise, stand for nothing and must be swept aside as betrayers of the cause. 'Violence is the way of the world he declared and he said we must find our allies where we can – even sometimes with those others might think are enemies. 'Sometimes', he said, 'against a common foe, our enemies are our friends. Then the fight between good and evil can advance unimpeded by the weak who seek a middle way of compromise.'"

"This man repeated his loathing of President Johnson. Then we discussed what might be done to end his meddling.

"At the end of our visit, he told me a package would be delivered to me with instructions the next day. It arrived and I followed the instructions closely.

"And so we disposed of our common foe."

Agent Bone, seeing the obsessed young man wanting to tell his story his own way and in his own words, waited for him to finish his monologue.

"I learned of the catering service and became employed so I could complete my mission. This I did."

To make the point clear, and as Ahmed clearly felt he'd finished his story. Bone added, "so you killed the former President?"

"Yes, I killed the great Satan, Johnson."

Not exactly the words he was looking for, but they would do, Bone thought. So who was the American official who supplied the instrument of assassination?

He didn't have to wait long to find out.

"And this is why I tell you my story.

"The American official who gave me the tool I needed was from the highest levels of your government. He proved how divided and corrupt you all have become. You turn upon yourselves and look to us to finish the work you are too timid or weak to do yourselves. This man told me he had made other arrangements to eliminate Johnson, but wasn't sure the person he contacted would have the courage to do it. He needed me to assure the deed got done."

Bone probed, "And this high government official – how did you know you weren't being led into a trap?"

"He was too high – he wouldn't stoop to such things. He obviously figured we would claim credit and he would escape responsibility altogether. What he foolishly failed to consider is that we would see his actions as a badge of honor for our cause and proof for us to publish that we even have our enemies rushing to help us."

"How high was this official?"

"He formerly counseled presidents. I believe you called him a 'National Security Adviser'. He was even on the radio program of that cowardly cur, Charlie Gasser, the day after the President's death."

Rod Churlish, Bone thought to himself! Meeting in person with a terrorist? How could he even consider doing such a thing, much less be so careless? Apparently Churlish had figured that if the crime were detected, as Ahmed suggested, those committing it would claim credit and not want to share the glory with an infidel. Alternately, Johnson's death would be taken as natural and that would be the end of it. Either way, Churlish would have gotten rid of Joshua Johnson.

What he didn't bargain on was his co-conspirators seeing his treachery as a defection to their side and proof of the depravity of the Western way of life. So far so good, but Bone had to nail it down.

"So you're telling me the former National Security Advisor, Rod Churlish gave you the electronic device you used to kill President Johnson?" Bone said these words with a deliberate and calculated skepticism in his voice.

"Yes, exactly." Ahmed replied with an even coolness that was chilling.

CHAPTER 25

CLOSURE

Now not one, but two paths had led to Churlish's doorstep and from widely different sources. A warrant was issued for his arrest. Adding insult to injury, the federal court judge, at the urging of Agent U.S. Attorney McCloud, denied Churlish bail because of his prospect of fleeing the country.

The news sparked a bombshell of media attention. How could someone who held himself out as such a bastion of patriotism have had a hand not only in an assassination plot of a former U.S. President, but one involving collaboration with Mideastern terrorists as well?

And the link with Charlie Gasser - proven by wire transfers to Saudi accounts linked to terrorist organizations - still seemed incredible. Yet, Bone reflected, there was Gasser, scrambling to save his tail and, at least for the duration of his criminal proceeding, deprived of his radio pulpit. Stations across the country dropped his broadcasts like the poison apple he'd become given the charges against him.

Churlish still maintained a defiant silence, preferring to respond through his attorneys. And, like Gasser's counsel, Churlish, of course, invoked all the same procedural safeguards afforded criminal defendants which he had for years condemned as "coddling criminals".

Secret Service Agent, Dick Rodman, became a critical link in the government's case. His testimony tied Gasser, Churlish, and the electronic device, into the plot to assassinate Johnson. He also described his effort to thwart the plot, a move clearly anticipated by Churlish, who'd set up his backup plan with Muhammad Ahmed. The combination of the two plots ultimately proved successful in accomplishing the assassination of the former president.

Among Churlish's greatest miscalculations was his involvement with Ahmed. He appeared shocked and chagrined when his former conspirator turned on him and almost gleefully cited Churlish's treachery as proof of "bankrupt Western civilization".

Churlish appeared, to those close to him, to be equally chagrined that instead of eliminating President Johnson and his agenda, the plot elevated him globally to hero status as a martyr for reform.

But few remained close to Churlish, as the facts of the case leaked out over the weeks following.

Those on the political right felt betrayed, and lined up on Meet the Press, Washington Week In Review, and Fox News to vilify the former National Security Advisor for his apparent treachery and betrayal of his country. One could hardly ignore two more contrasting eyewitnesses than a decorated former Secret Service Agent and a self-proclaimed Islamic terrorist.

Charlie Gasser, meanwhile, attempting to save something of his former media domain, loudly claimed as his defense that he was pressured by Churlish to a heartfelt belief he was "doing the right thing" for America. This time, it appeared even he had gone too far. His hypocrisy came written on the records of his bank transfer to the Saudi terrorist factions and communications with Churlish about "eliminating" the enemy. Gasser became a popular butt of late night television jokes.

The O'Brien Administration, formerly close to Churlish and embracing him on its security team, made clear they would do everything in their power to assure the Justice Department prosecuted the case against him to the fullest extent of the law. Because of possible conflicts, they requested appointment of a Special Prosecutor to handle the case. Given his active role in uncovering the crime, this regrettably took Bill McCloud off the case.

In the wake of these developments, political winds shifted even more decisively away from confrontation and towards a more cooperative approach to the environment and global initiatives. In addition, President O'Brien seemed truly grieved at the death of his former political adversary and recent ally, Joshua Johnson, and was intent on vindicating this friendship.

Special Agent Bone, completing his investigation and turning it over to the Justice Department, found himself in the limelight he so detested. He did experience one consolation: his efforts prompted a profusely grateful call from Lydia Stonecraft. On an impulsive moment, he asked her if she cared to join him at a symphony concert in Grand Rapids when she was next in town, and she accepted.

EPILOGUE

Charlie Gasser's attorneys did a good job, considering the charges he faced including conspiracy to assassinate a former President, criminal transactions with prohibited foreign entities, lying to interfere with a criminal investigation, and involvement in the actual assassination of a president. His attorney secured a mandatory twenty year prison sentence followed by ten years probation on reduced charges, with the twenty year sentence to be served at a minimum security facility. This was a big relief to Gasser because of his deep fear of the abusive treatment he might experience at the hands of other prisoners. He hoped the chances of "getting poked and prodded" as he put it, would be less in a minimum security prison,

To get such favorable treatment, he was expected to "sing" for the prosecutors. This he did willingly, providing the Special Prosecutors with veritable serenade of useful information with which to go after Rod Churlish and Dick Rodman.

However, the story he told also projected such a hypocritical and cowardly person, that no broadcast media would touch his story. This may have been relatively meaningless to Gasser since the federal judge imposed as a condition of his sentence that in addition to a substantial fine, Gasser would forfeit any proceeds on any book or other productions concerning his involvement in the conspiracy; the proceeds of which would go to the U.S. Institute of Environmental

Synergy in Washington, D.C., the Institute modeled after President Johnson's final paper.

Former National Security Advisor, Rod Churlish, in contrast to his former co-conspirator, defiantly maintained his innocence of all charges. So insistent was he despite evidence from multiple sources, that his attorneys argued among themselves whether to present a defense of insanity or at least diminished capacity, on the theory that their client had become so obsessed with eliminating the former President he was no longer of sound mind. Churlish's explosive and expletive-filled rejection of this idea forced them to pursue the "naïve jury" strategy. This basically depended on the hope that they could convince at least one of a carefully screened panel of twelve jurors that in spite of all the evidence, there was still a reasonable doubt their client had not conspired to kill the former President, or to concoct the backup plan to accomplish his objective.

The strategy failed. The former National Security Advisor to U.S. Presidents wound up convicted of the same charges as the fanatic Jihadist Mohammed Ahmed, who rejecting a court-appointed counsel, chose to represent himself.

In large part because of lack of remorse by either defendant, each was sentenced to life in prison without possibility of parole. The Judge, in an ironic twist of justice, directed they serve their sentence in the same maximum security federal prison, where they could be regularly reminded of one another's treachery. Churlish also forfeited his government pension and any right to exploit his story commercially.

Former Secret Service Agent, Dick Rodman, received a five year sentence in a minimum security facility, with five years' probation and forfeiture of any government pension. His distinguished government service record and the heartfelt remorse he experienced for his hand in the plot and his efforts to subvert it, together with his cooperation in the investigation, weighed heavily in his favor. Upon discharge from prison he sought dual employment, working part time in a V.A. facility in Detroit, counseling veterans suffering from post traumatic stress disorder, and part time aiding local community groups to apply Template principles through creating community gardens, educational programs and recycling projects.

Special Agent Derrick Bone, vaulted to a celebrity status like that of Elliot Ness in an earlier era, received multiple offers for speaking engagements, and even a movie deal. He turned them all down, as he did an offer to take over directorship of the Chicago F.B.I. office. Bone knew himself well enough to know these offers would merely take him away from investigating crimes. That was what he knew best and what he most enjoyed - at least as much as he found it possible to enjoy anything.

One thing he did enjoy that attended his conclusion of the Johnson murder investigation was time spent with Professor Lydia Stonecraft. A common interest in classical music and strenuous sports complimented a certain ferocity of purpose each possessed in pursing their convictions. Regrettably for Bone, Stonecraft's schedule after her mentor's death became even more frenetic. Speaking engagements, requests for consultations on implementing the Template, and her own scientific and political endeavors made their visits few and far between. So Bone largely resumed his "life of a monk crossed with that of a worker bee."

The O'Brien Administration in addition to its full support of the investigation and prosecution of those implicated in the former President's death, made good on President O'Brien's' commitment to his late friend by aggressively pushing for implementation of the Template in the policies of his administration. He pushed for long term tax incentives to encourage private industry to develop products earning high marks under <u>Template</u> principles. And he encouraged the government to form <u>regional </u>Institutes of Environmental Synergy across America, in a wave of creative competition to figure out ways to better live in harmony with the environment.

Joshua Johnson's legacy – in promoting the Template principles and establishing Institutes of Environmental Synergy around the world - continued to grow. The problems so long in the making weren't going to be solved overnight. And with each added natural disaster, the need for change became more evident.

But in the words of the late President, invoking Abraham Lincoln, the world had finally begun to "think anew and act anew".

Whether change could come fast enough or reach far enough, only history would reveal.

THE BEGINNING.

51096323R00096

Made in the USA
Lexington, KY
12 April 2016